CARL & JERRY

Their *Complete* Adventures
from *Popular Electronics*

By John T. Frye W9EGV

Volume 1: October 1954 - December 1956

CwP

Copperwood Press • Scottsdale, Arizona

To the Eternal Memory
of the Grand Old Men
of Hobby Electronics:

Herb S. Brier W9EGQ 1914 - 1977
Lou Garner 1914 - 2004
and, of course,
John T. Frye W9EGV

ISBN-10: 1-932084-21-5
ISBN-13: 978-1-932084-21-4

COPPERWOOD MEDIA, LLC
SCOTTSDALE, ARIZONA

Table of Contents

Introduction

Toward the end of 1954, a brand-new magazine appeared, and changed the face of hobby electronics forever. *Popular Electronics* was created by Ziff-Davis Publishing in New York City, and premiered with the October 1954 issue. *Popular Electronics* was revolutionary for a simple reason: Before it appeared, "hobby electronics" was basically synonymous with "radio." There had been magazines devoted to hobby radio (both ham radio and radio listening, tinkering, and repair) for over 25 years. But in the decade following World War II, electronics absolutely exploded, and spread from the radio ghetto into TV, high-fidelity audio, and a jungle of gadgetry like Geiger counters, fire alarms, photographic light meters, and on and on and on. Electronics was not simply radio anymore. Cheap war surplus tubes and components were a glut on the market, and a whole new generation of young tinkerers were flexing their muscles and seeing just how far beyond radio they could go.

And there on page 38 was something else: A piece of fiction. Under the title "A New Company Is Launched" was a 2,500 word short story about two teenage boys who discover that they share the love of electron-pushing. The short, fat one was a slide-rule ace. The tall, thin one with the Far Side glasses was good with tools. On page 38, Theory met Practice, and a legend was born.

For the next ten years, John T. Frye spun tales around Carl Anderson and Jerry Bishop. The boys got wild ideas, built things, and had adventures. Better still, they explained what they were doing, and how it worked. The Carl and Jerry stories were a species of tutorial fiction, somewhere between Tom Swift and a Cleveland Institute of Electronics correspondence course. Details were sparse, but the broad strokes were always there, and as the series went on, the boys regularly referred to projects that had been published as articles in earlier issues. (I'll bet this shrewd marketing move converted more than a few isolated newsstand sales to regular subscriptions!)

But best of all is that they showed a whole generation of young people that electronics was *fun*, it was comprehensible, and even respectable. Young tinkerers saw themselves in Carl and Jerry, who ignited countless dreams of putting iron to solder and creating something that may not have existed before. More than a few people have told me that Carl and Jerry launched them into successful careers in science and engineering. "They made it sound maybe a little too easy," one recalled in a recent email, "but that just made me work harder so I could succeed like they did. It worked."

Boy, did it.

About John T. Frye himself not much is known, though I continue to search for details about his life. Most of what we know cooks down to this: He was a writer and a skilled service tech. He was from Indiana. And, amazingly, he spent much or all of his life in a wheelchair. In addition to a couple of books on radio/TV repair he wrote a column called "Mac's Service Shop" in *Electronics World*, another Ziff-Davis publication, which catered more to the electronics industry than to hobbyists. (Do you know more about John than this? Please drop me a note, to jduntemann@copperwood.com.)

The first *Popular Electronics* magazines are now well over half a century old, and they have begun crumbling to mold and dust. (Their corner of my library carries that unmistakable whiff of damp basement.) In the summer of 2006, my friend Michael Covington suggested that Carl and Jerry could be rescued and made available both to their old friends who "knew them when" as well as hobbyists who had not yet been born when the series concluded in late 1964. We knew who held the *Popular Electronics* copyrights, and after some inquiries I graciously received permission from Larry Steckler of PopTronics to gather the 119 Carl and Jerry stories into anthologies, of which this is the first of five. All five have now been published, and are available from Amazon as paperbacks.

I've created a Web page devoted to Carl and Jerry, which contains an index of all 119 stories, with brief descriptions of each so that if you recall a favorite Carl and Jerry adventure, you can determine when it was originally published and in which anthology it appears.

http://www.copperwood.com/carlandjerry.htm

Many thanks to Larry Steckler for allowing us to do this, and to Michael Covington and his wife Melody (along with numerous other people) for offering help and sage advice. The project has been a tremendous amount of fun, and, egad! I've begun building things in the basement again. This stuff is *catching.*

Get acquainted with Carl and Jerry again—or for the first time—and see if you don't get caught too!

Jeff Duntemann K7JPD, Editor
Scottsdale, Arizona,
June 10, 2023

A NEW COMPANY IS LAUNCHED

October 1954

Jerry Bishop was in his basement "laboratory," but the teenager was not exactly laboring. Instead, with his well-padded frame stretched out comfortably on a leather couch, his dark crew-cut pillowed on his clasped hands, and his round face staring vacantly up at the ceiling, he was listening blissfully to Patti Page inviting him to "Cross Over The Bridge." The invitation was being issued by a spinning record on a player resting on the floor beside the couch. The throbbing volume that issued from a speaker cabinet in the corner was just barely below the threshold of pain.

Suddenly, riding over Patti's dulcet tones, there came a strong youthful voice saying with great deliberation, "One, two, three, four test. This is W9EGV testing. One, two, three, four."

"That's not on the record," was Jerry's brilliant muttered deduction. He heaved himself to his feet and walked over to the phono-amplifier sitting on a workbench and turned it off. The voice dropped in volume, but it did not disappear. Instead its source switched from the speaker to the open basement window.

Determined to get to the bottom of the mystery, Jerry padded up the outside basement steps and stood in the back yard listening. The voice clearly came from an open upstairs window of the house next door, a house into which new neighbors had just moved the day before. As Jerry stared upward, debating his next move, a boy's reddish-tinted curly blond head popped out of the window. He was holding a microphone in his hand and was looking upward at a wire that ran from the top of the window frame to a tree back near the alley.

"Hey, you, what do you think you're doing?" Jerry demanded.

The head in the window turned and stared disinterestedly down at Jerry with a pair of bright blue eyes behind horn-rimmed glasses.

"I don't 'think'; I *know* what I'm doing," the boy in the window replied coldly. "I'm seeing if my amateur transmitter will load up this new antenna I've put up."

"As loud as you were yelling, you wouldn't need a transmitter," Jerry observed tartly.

"I wouldn't have to yell if some dope wasn't running his platter-player wide open. Was that you?"

"Never mind that," Jerry said hastily, "What I want to know is how come I'm picking up what you say into that microphone on my record player?"

"Are you?" the new boy said with quick interest. "Wait a minute and I'll be over."

In a few seconds he burst out the back door and vaulted easily over the low fence between the yards. His tall, lean, well-muscled figure was clothed in a pair of baggy-pocketed army fatigue pants and a torn sweat shirt.

"My name's Carl Anderson," he offered. "Guess we're neighbors. What's your handle?"

"Handle?" Jerry repeated with a puzzled look.

"Sure; I mean your name. That's ham talk."

"Oh, I'm Jerry Bishop. Come on down into my lab, and I'll show you the player."

As the two boys stepped inside the basement door, Carl stopped and took a searching look around. The first thing that caught his eye was the fine wide workbench that ran clear across one end of the room. On a board above the bench was a miscellaneous collection of hand tools. Carl walked over and disapprovingly ran a finger along the edge of a snaggle-toothed handsaw and inspected a pair of screwdrivers with broken, twisted bits and battered handles. Then he turned his attention to the amplifier sitting on the end of the bench and followed with his eye a long line from the amplifier to the record player sitting on the floor by the couch across the room. Another line went from the amplifier to what looked as though it might be a birdhouse for an ostrich, sitting over in a corner of the room.

"That's my bass-reflex cabinet," Jerry announced. "I built it myself."

Carl walked over to the crude speaker cabinet and examined it closely.

"Did you really manage to saw those boards that crooked or have you got a pet beaver that gnaws them off like that?" he inquired disparagingly.

"So I can't saw straight!" Jerry admitted with a good natured grin; "but take a listen."

As he said this, he turned on the amplifier. The whole basement was flooded with a sea of music. The volume was so great that the whumping of the bass drum actually made the tools jangle on the tool board.

Carl strode over and turned the volume down to a mere roar.

"It doesn't sound too bad," he grudgingly admitted, "but I'll never know why. I never saw a more haywire layout. That long lead from the player to the amplifier is what's picking up my signal. Wait until I get my solder gun and a capacitor and we'll see if we can cure it."

He took the cellar steps two at a time as he said this; and Jerry, exhausted by the sight of so much energy, sank back on the couch to await his return. He did not have long to wait, for in a minute Carl was back, carrying a device that looked like a Buck Rogers ray gun in one hand and a little brown Bakelite object with two wire leads coming out of it in the other. In a flash he had the amplifier turned over and was probing around in the wiring with the tip of the solder gun, explaining as he went:

"The trouble is caused by the strong signal from my transmitter collecting on the input element of the first amplifier tube."

"You mean on the grid?" Jerry asked.

Carl shot a surprised look at him and went on, "That's right. This strong radio frequency signal upsets the normal operating conditions of the tube and makes the amplifier act more like a radio receiver than a plain amplifier. I'm going to connect this small condenser—

capacitor is a more accurate name—between the grid of the first tube and the chassis so that signals from my transmitter will be bypassed to ground..."

"And then," Jerry smoothly interrupted, "the grid will no longer be swung positive on peaks, grid rectification will stop, and the tube will cease to be biased by grid leak action to the point where it acts as a detector."

"Hey, where'd you learn that electronic jive?" Carl demanded. "You got a ham ticket?"

"Nope," Jerry answered, vastly pleased at the impression he had made on his new neighbor. " And don't be afraid I'll steal too much of your thunder." He walked over to a bookshelf on the wall that, in contrast to the workbench, was in perfect order. On it were a few books of elementary physics and several stacks of radio magazines.

"I get a large charge out of reading anything about electricity or electronics," he explained. "It just happens that the last issue of the magazines in this stack contained an explanation of how radio signals could cause interference to audio amplifiers; so that is why I had that one little item down so pat."

"Well, all right," Carl remarked as he finished soldering in the capacitor and turned the amplifier on. "We hams get so used to people not understanding what we're talking about that it makes us feel funny when we hear a stranger spouting our lingo. Now let's try this thing. Leave the needle off the record and keep listening at different positions of the gain control. I'll dash over and turn on the rig and put out a test."

As he said the last word he was already halfway up the steps. Soon Jerry could hear his voice coming faintly through the basement window; but no setting of the amplifier gain control caused the voice to be heard in the speaker.

"The operation is a success, Doctor," he yelled out the window. "Come on back.

"Say," he remarked as Carl came back into the basement and perched himself on the workbench, "what was that you were saying about seeing if your transmitter would 'load up' your new antenna ?"

"That's right. This antenna is cut for 3950 kilocycles, according to my figuring, and I wanted to make sure it would take energy from the transmitter."

"What would keep it from doing that?"

"Being the wrong length. A transmitting antenna has to be the proper length so that it will resonate at the frequency of the transmitter before it will accept power from the transmitter."

"How do you calculate the proper length?"

"There's a formula for it, but I just use a table in the *Radio Amateur's Handbook*. It says the proper length is 118 feet and six inches."

"Don't you wonder about the reasons behind those tables?" Jerry asked curiously.

"Not me. I just want to know how things work, not why. All I know is that an antenna should be roughly a half wavelength long for good transmission or reception of a given frequency."

"H-m-m," Jerry reflected. "That reminds me of sound waves. I remember in physics class we found that if an open-ended tube was to be resonant at the frequency of a tuning fork, it had to be a half wavelength long at the fork's frequency. Just for kicks, let's see if radio and sound waves can be handled the same way. First off, if we divide the speed of a wave motion by the frequency of the waves, we get the length of each wave; right?"

Carl wrinkled his brow in deep concentration. "I guess so," he finally agreed hesitatingly. "If we knew how many feet a minute a freight train was moving and divided that by the number of identical cars that passed in a minute, we'd get the length of each car. I guess it would be the same with waves."

"Exactly. We also know that light and radio waves scamper along at a speed of 300,000,000 meters per second, and we have the frequency you are shooting at as being 3950 kilocycles or 3,950,000 cycles per second. Check?"

"Double check," Carl agreed. "We can lop those three ciphers off each number and divide 300,000 by 3950. You got a pencil and piece of paper?"

Without answering Jerry dug down in the litter of papers and books piled on the end of the couch and came up with a cheap and battered slide rule which he began to manipulate with a few extra flourishes strictly for the benefit of his guest.

"The answer," he finally announced with all the importance of a Supreme Court Judge handing down a fateful decision, "is very close to 76 meters."

"We're getting warm!" Carl said excitedly. "This band I'm working is called the 75 Meter Phone Band."

"Since your antenna is going to be a half wavelength long, we chop seventy-six in two and get thirty-eight meters," Jerry continued. "A foot equals .3048 meter; so we divide 38 by .3048, and the good old slip-stick says…" he paused to work the slide rule again, "…exactly 124.5 feet," he finished weakly.

"The good old slip-stick or the guy slipping it must have slipped," Carl jeered. "That's too far off 118.5 feet to be right-say!" he suddenly broke off as he struck his forehead with a clenched fist, "I remember reading somewhere that a half wavelength resonant conductor is always somewhat shorter than an actual half wavelength in free space. It's shorter by about 5%. Try taking 5% off that and see what you get."

"Five percent of 124.5 is close to six feet, and 124.5 feet minus 6 gives us precisely 118.5 feet," Jerry announced triumphantly.

"Whew! I'm glad that's over," Carl said as he bent forward and mopped his face with the slack in the front of his sweatshirt. "This brain wrestling is harder on me than playing in a double overtime game."

He and Jerry grinned at each other with the mutual satisfaction that comes from having joined in a successful operation.

"Say," Carl began hesitantly, "I've got an idea, but if you don't like it, just say so. My feelings won't be hurt. Here's the way I look at it: both of us are interested in electronics. You like to read and think about it; I like to experiment and build things. You've got a dandy place to work but not much equipment. I've got a ham station, a volt-ohmmeter, and a whole box I of radio parts, but no place to work except my bedroom. You're good on math and theory where I am weak, but you don't seem too good with tools—"

"Let's face it: I'm about as clever as a cow on a crutch with tools," Jerry admitted, without shame.

"I like tools and like to work with them," Carl went on. "To cut it short, how's about our sort of joining forces and working together? Maybe I'm wrong, but I think it would be a lot of fun. But if you don't like the idea—" ,

"I'm with you!" Jerry exclaimed. "A hobby is twice as much fun when you've got someone to work and argue with. As far as I'm concerned, we're in business. What'll we call ourselves? It's got to be something that sounds serious and imposing."

"Natch," Carl agreed. "How about 'Electronic Experimenters, Inc.'?"

"Let's change that 'Inc.' to 'Ltd.' " Jerry suggested. "Somehow it sounds more swanky."

"Fine! I'll get out my mechanical drawing set and make up a sign for over the basement door tonight," Carl said with mounting enthusiasm.

For a minute the two stood looking at each other, half serious, half joking. Then Jerry stuck out his hand. "Want to shake on it, Pardner?"

Instantly his plump hand was grasped by Carl's sinewy fingers.

"Here's to 'Electronic Experimenters, Ltd.'"   —30—

A LIGHT SUBJECT

November 1954

Carl Anderson entered his home in his usual forceful manner. That is, he took a giant step across the threshold and clung tightly to the doorknob until the slamming door stopped him in mid-stride. He next dog-trotted down the hall to the open door of the living room where he stopped briefly to execute a graceful push-shot with his schoolbooks to the davenport cushions. Finally he sailed into the kitchen like a whirling dervish. With almost a continuous motion he jerked open the refrigerator door, lifted out a pint bottle of chocolate milk, downed it with four or five thirsty gulps, and banged the door shut. The empty bottle went into the sink with a jangling clatter as the boy slammed out the back door.

Upstairs in her sewing room, Mrs. Anderson listened to the progress of this miniature door-slamming tornado through the downstairs part of her house without any particular sign of annoyance. In the first place, she was used to it; and in the second, she experienced that warm feeling of contentment a mother always knows when her children, be they four or forty years of age, are safely home. Even though Carl had gone out the back door she knew he was headed no farther than the basement "laboratory" of his friend, Jerry Bishop, next door.

As Carl skipped down the outside basement steps and burst through the door, his eyes were met by a singular sight. Jerry's well-padded form was sprawled on the couch at one side of the room. Although it was still broad daylight, he held a lighted flashlight in his hand and was waving the narrow beam languidly back and forth across the face of what looked like a small birdhouse sitting on the workbench along the opposite wall. Each time the spot of light

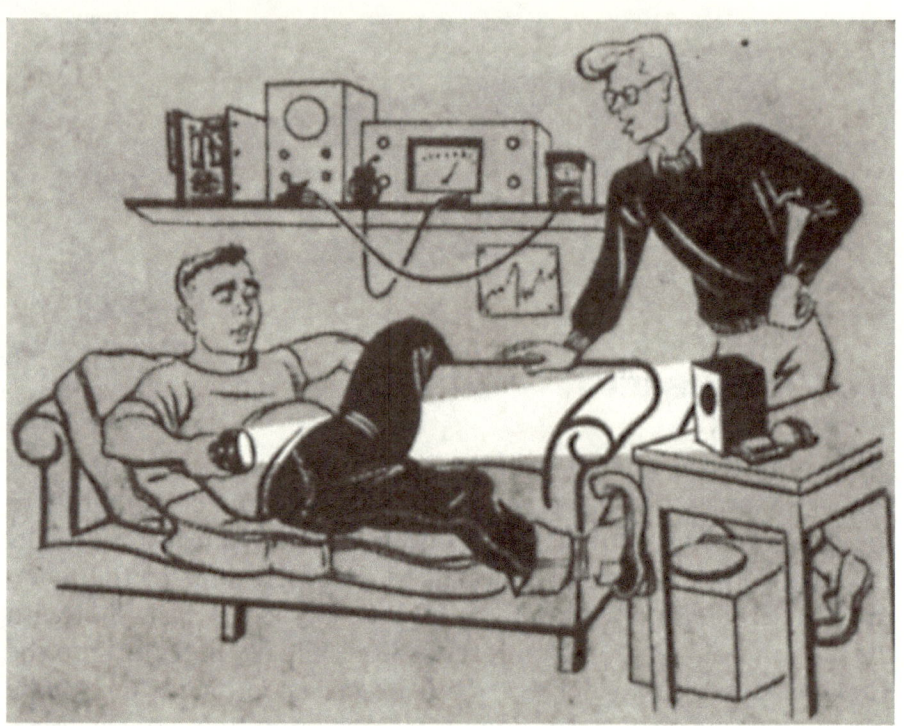

passed over the quarter-sized opening in the face of this box, an electric bell lying on the bench beside it gave out with a brief "br-r-r-ing" of sound.

Carl slumped against the doorjamb and said lugubriously, "I've been afraid of this. The mad genius has finally flipped his lid. That's what comes of reading physics texts and tube manuals instead of comic books like any other red-blooded American boy. I'm a little disappointed, though, in the lack of originality. Old Diogenes used that carrying-a-light-in-the-daytime routine several centuries ago."

"That's our boy!" Jerry murmured as he grinned across at Carl. "If you can't understand it, belittle it, is the motto, huh? Had you not been so busy trying to lash your feeble intellect into thinking up a wisecrack about the flashlight, you might have noticed some connection between my moving its beam back and forth and the ringing of the bell."

"So-o-o-o," Carl drawled with quizzically arched eyebrows.

"So I'm experimenting with photoelectric cells. Notice that as long as I keep the beam of light on the cell through that small opening in the box the bell continues to ring, but it stops as soon as the light is turned away."

"Say, how about that! That's pretty neat!" Carl said with sudden enthusiasm. "Let me do it. How does it work?" he asked as Jerry let him take the flashlight and play it back and forth across the opening in the box.

"You really want to know or are you just asking to be polite?"

"I really want to know, Stupid!" Carl growled, "and you're just aching to lecture; so quit stalling and get on with it."

"Okay, but first I've got to know if you remember anything at all of what you learned in physics about the construction of an atom."

"Of course I remember," Carl said indignantly. "An atom has a positive nucleus about which circle tiny negative do-jiggers of electricity called electrons. There are always just enough of these electrons in a normal atom so that their total negative charge is equal to the positive charge of the nucleus, leaving the atom with a neutral charge. Under some circumstances, though, an electron can be pried loose from its atom and go bucketing around by itself. An atom that has lost an electron assumes a positive charge and is called an ion. Electrons are attracted to any positively charged object; ions have a yen for negatively charged things."

"You amaze me!" Jerry remarked as he lifted up the lid of the box on the bench and pulled out a small glass photoelectric cell. "You can see this cell only has two elements in it. That half-cylinder is the cathode, and the little rod in the middle is the anode. Notice the inside surface of the semi-cylinder is coated with a kind of silvery-colored gunk. The stuff may be one of several different substances, but whatever one is used in this particular tube, its main characteristic is that electrons are given off from its surface whenever light falls upon it. Up to a certain point, the more light that falls on this cathode coating the more electrons are emitted."

"What's inside the bulb besides the cathode and anode?"

"Mostly plenty of nothing. Maintaining a high vacuum inside the bulb greatly aids the emission of electrons from the cathode and helps them cross over to the anode."

"Why do they go to the anode?"

"Because it is positively charged with respect to the cathode. You will remember you told me a positively-charged object has a great attraction for free electrons. In this case the anode is ninety volts positive with respect to the cathode, and there is a steady stream of electrons from the cathode to the anode. Any time you have a stream of electrons all moving in the same direction you have an electrical current, for an electric current is made up of a movement of electrons. Before I forget it, I had better mention that while this particular tube is of the high vacuum type, some photoelectric cells have a controlled amount of gas inside the bulb."

"What's the idea?"

"It increases the sensitivity. Let me think how I can explain this. Oh yes, now I've got it. Did you ever see an apple fall from the very tiptop of a tree heavily loaded with dead-ripe fruit?"

"Suppose I have, but what's that got to do with photocells?"

"Perhaps you noticed that on the way down the falling apple struck other apples and dislodged them so they fell with it. The branches on which these apples had been clinging jerked upward as they were freed of the weight of the dislodged fruit, and this movement knocked loose still more apples from the branches above them. The net result could easily be a dozen apples falling to the ground as the result of the loosening of that first apple from its stem.

"The same thing happens inside the gas type photoelectric cell. As an electron is scampering merrily along toward the anode, it collides with a gas atom and knocks loose one or more electrons from the atom that immediately join it on its short and speedy journey. The gas atom, converted into an ion by the loss of an electron, is attracted to the cathode. As it falls into the cathode the smash knocks loose still more electrons that are then free to go to the anode. Just as happened with the apples, for every electron that is freed from the cathode by the influence of light falling upon it, a half-dozen or so electrons may reach the anode. This greatly increases the sensitivity of the cell."

"Then why aren't all photoelectric cells of the gas type?"

"A shrewd question, *Carlos mi amigo*, but there is an answer: while gas cells have a higher sensitivity than vacuum types, the latter have higher internal resistance, maintain a more constant sensitivity throughout their life, and are not so easily damaged by applying higher than rated voltages."

"How come you've got other parts in this box? I see another tube in here besides a relay and a bunch of resistors. Why don't you just put the relay that turns the bell on and off in the anode circuit of the photoelectric cell and let the current flowing through the cell open and close it?"

"Because the current through the cell is very tiny, being measured in microamperes. A relay that would work on such a tiny current would be very delicate and undependable. It is much better to employ some sort of current amplifying tube between the cell and the relay. That tube you see in, there is one particularly suited for this job, and is called a *thyratron*."

"What the heck's a thyratron? Sounds like a glandular disease."

"Well, it's not. A thyratron is sometimes called a relay tube because its action is very much like that of a relay. As long as the negative potential on the grid of such a tube remains above a certain critical value, no current at all flows through the plate circuit of the tube; but when the negative grid voltage is lowered to that critical value, the plate current suddenly rises from zero to a comparatively high value. If we adjust the grid voltage of a thyratron very close to the critical value and then arrange for the current through our photoelectric cell to influence this grid potential, very slight changes in illumination of the cell can produce rapid and positive operation of a relay in the plate circuit of the thyratron tube. Photoelectric cells and thyratrons go together like hot dogs and root beer."

"Are there any other kinds of photoelectric cells besides the vacuum and gas types?"

"Sure thing. Both of these are what are known as 'emissive' types. In addition we have the 'conductive' type of cell. This cell has two electrodes connected by a material that exhibits a change in resistance in accordance with the light falling on it. A typical cell will display 30 megohms of resistance in the dark and only one megohm in bright sunlight. Such a cell behaves much the same as the emissive type with this exception: It displays no polarity and is less subject to damage by high voltages. Conductive cells may or may not be mounted in a vacuum, for low pressure is not necessary for their proper action."

"What kind of a cell would be in the light meter my dad uses when he takes pictures?"

"That's still another type called the 'generative' cell. In many ways, particularly at this time, it is the most interesting of the lot. Several materials, including selenium, when spread in a thin film on a metal disc actually generate electrical energy under the stimulus of light. This energy appears between the outer surface of the film and the metal disc. The current put out by one of these photovoltaic cells is polarized and can be employed to deflect a sensitive meter. That is what is done in the exposure meter you mention. A selenium cell, sensitive micro-ammeter, and a calibrating resistor are connected together so that the meter reading indicates the foot-candles of light falling on the cell window."

"Why do you say these cells are the most interesting 'particularly at this time'?"

"For one thing these cells convert light energy directly into electrical energy without first going through some other form, such as heat. That has tremendous and exciting significance. Every single day the sun bathes the earth in more than 1,000,000,000,000,000 kilowatt hours of energy. This daily gift of radiated energy is equal to all that is contained in the world's reserves of coal, oil, natural gas, *and uranium*. The sad part of it is, though, that practically all of this energy goes to waste, at least as far as man's attempt to harness it is concerned. Your dad's photo-electric exposure meter represents about the best we have been able to do in converting light into electricity until very recently, and it has an efficiency of only about one percent.

"Just a few months ago, however, the same Bell Laboratories that invented the transistor came up with a new solar energy converter that is six times as efficient as the light meter. Each cell in this converter is made up of a wafer of two types of specially treated silicon—the main ingredient of common sand. One of these silicon cells in full sunlight will produce about a half a volt with no load. When the load is adjusted to take maximum power, the voltage falls to about one-third of a volt and stays close to that figure over a wide range of illumination. A short-circuited cell in bright sunlight will deliver about one-eighth of an ampere for each square inch of active surface or about one-tenth ampere at a load causing a one-third volt output. Groups of cells can be connected in parallel for additional current or in series for additional voltage. As long as this 'solar' battery is working into a high impedance load, good voltage output is had with much less than full illumination. On quite cloudy days the silicon cell will produce usable output with the radiation that comes from the sky."

"How much power have they managed to get out of thing?"

"Silicon solar batteries have been used to power transistorized radios and transmitters and to operate a toy ferris wheel. Telephone engineers are already thinking about using them to run low-power mobile equipment or as battery chargers for amplifiers in rural telephone systems. At present it takes a ten-cell battery to produce a quarter of a watt, and Bell engineers estimate you would need about twenty-five square feet of silicon wafer to keep a hundred-watt lamp burning and about a quarter of an acre of the stuff to power a small home.

"Keep in mind, though, that we have only just gotten a toe-hold in this field, and improved efficiencies are bound to appear. In fact the Wright Air Development Center of the Air Research and Development Command has already announced a new solar generator using cadmium sulphide instead of silicon, and it has been estimated that a thin crystal slab of this material with an area of only sixty square feet could be built into the roof of a house and would supply all its electrical requirements."

Carl stood up and stretched until his joints cracked. "That's the way it goes," he mourned. "No longer will I be able to draw a simple pleasure from watching the electric eye door at the super market swing open at my approach. Now I'll be thinking about thyratrons, electrons, silicon cells, and cadmium sulphide. Worse yet, when I'm trying to get a sun tan, I'll be feeling guilty about all that solar energy I'm squandering!"   —30—

THE HOT DOG CASE

December 1954

Jerry Bishop looked up from the transistor oscillator on which he had been working all evening as the door of his basement laboratory was flung violently back against the wall and his chum, Carl Anderson, entered. In one hand Carl carried a small rectangular box into which were plugged a pair of earphones worn loosely around his neck. The other hand firmly clutched the leather collar of a shaggy, stiff-legged Airedale who was obviously accompanying his master under considerable protest.

"Hiya, Carl," Jerry languidly greeted his neighbor. "What kind of a gadget is that? Don't tell me you have invented an electronic flea killer and are about to demonstrate it on poor old Bosco. Here, Bosco; here, boy."

"This thing is a radiation detector," Carl explained as he released the dog and hastily slammed the door shut to cut off his escape. "Aunt Ida out in Denver sent it to me. She says out there these days a person without some sort of Geiger counter feels as naked as a Westerner would have felt a hundred years ago without his shooting iron. But now I want to show you something. Put on these earphones."

As he said this he dragged the wall-eyed dog over to the bench and handed the phones to Jerry. A slow, erratic clicking sound could be heard in the phones, but as Carl unceremoniously grabbed up one of Bosco's front paws and thrust it near the box, the clicks suddenly increased in tempo, and a little neon lamp on the face of the box flashed in unison.

"See!" Carl said excitedly. "That gadget shows all four of Bosco's paws are hotter than a 110 volt lamp in a 220 socket!"

25

"Makes him a real hot dog, doesn't it?" Jerry murmured facetiously and then backed hastily away from the withering glance Carl directed at him.

"Don't try to be funny," Carl advised. "This is a serious business. If we can just find where Bosco is acquiring these hot tootsies, we may locate a big uranium deposit and become independently wealthy. Why, in a couple of weeks we may be rolling in bubble gum and comic books!"

"A fascinating prospect," Jerry observed disparagingly as he tried to conceal how impressed he really was with Carl's discovery. "Have you got any idea how old Torrid Toes here got that way?"

"Not much of one. I just happened to stumble on to his interesting condition the first night I had the detector while I was trying it out on everything in reach. All I know is that every evening Bosco takes off up the alley and. is gone for an hour or so, and when he comes back he winds up the radiation detector as he does now. After a while this radiation seems to die out until the next time he makes one of these mysterious disappearances, and then it is right back up there."

"Have you tried following him?"

In answer Carl turned around and displayed a large three-cornered rent in his trousers where a hip pocket used to be. "How else do you think I lost the seat of my pants?" he demanded. "I'll swear Bosco knew I was trying to follow him and deliberately made it tough on me. He ducked through holes in board fences, jumped over barbed wire, cut through gardens, and stopped every now and then and kicked dirt over his tracks. I was trying to follow him over-a fence when I suffered this pants casualty—which incidentally I don't think Mom's going to appreciate. I've been thinking about fastening a can of whitewash with a small hole in it around his neck so the whitewash will leak out and leave a trail I can follow."

"Perish the thought!" Jerry exclaimed. "Such a crude mechanical contrivance is not worthy of a member of Electronic Experimenters, Ltd. On top of that, it might lead some curious busybody to our uranium lode. No, we must solve this mystery electronically."

"Such as how?"

"It's coming to me," Jerry said as he looked through Carl with the out-of-focus stare of a crystal gazer. "Have you still got the dry batteries we used to power your little communications receiver during the radio club's hidden transmitter hunt last month—and the shielded loop we used?"

"Yep, but if you're thinking of loading forty or fifty pounds of transmitter on old Bosco here, that's out. Pound for pound, he's as tough as any dog in the neighborhood—and maybe a little tougher—but he's no St. Bernard."

"Relax, Buster," Jerry said as he picked up a little clear plastic box not much larger than a package of chewing gum. "Do you think he can stagger along under this load?"

"Don't tell me that's a transmitter!"

For a reply Jerry switched on a small broadcast receiver above the workbench and tuned it to a station on the low frequency end of the band. Then he held the plastic box near the receiver and carefully adjusted a small screw protruding from one side of the box. As he did so, a heterodyning whistle swished down on the station being heard in the radio and, as it came to zero beat, completely blotted out the reception.

"Well I'll be darned," Carl marveled. "That little cuss surely puts out a sock with only one tiny hearing-aid battery for a power supply. But I didn't think transistors could be made to work at radio frequencies."

"The first ones couldn't, but now they have new 'intrinsic-barrier' type transistors that are capable of operating up to 400 megacycles. Even this garden-variety junction transistor I'm using will oscillate nicely over the entire broadcast band. We can set it for a dead spot at the low end of the band and then pick it up on the loop antenna for a distance of several yards, yet with no radiating antenna it won't put out enough signal to violate the FCC's regulations concerning such devices."

"How are we going to carry the receiver, loop, and batteries?"

"I've figured that out, too, but I want it to be a surprise. You bring all the stuff and Bosco over right after school tomorrow evening, and I'll show you," Jerry said as he switched off the receiver and started clearing off the bench for the night.

When Carl and Bosco entered the laboratory the next evening, the former stopped dead in his tracks at the sight of a king-size baby buggy standing in the middle of the room.

"Oh no, not that!" he groaned. "I'll die before I'll be caught pushing that overgrown perambulator up and down the street loaded with radio gear. Think what would happen if some of the high school gang caught us doing it. They'd get out the net for sure. Where did you ever get such a monstrosity, anyway?"

"It belongs to a cousin who used it for her twins. When she moved away from town she stored it in our attic. It's built like a Mack truck and will be just the ticket to carry the receiver and batteries. Aw, Carl, come on! Don't be stuffy. After all, we'll be going up and down the alleys, and it will be dark. Anyway, scientists like us can't be worried about what people may think."

"Well, all right," Carl agreed reluctantly; "but I'm warning you right now that the first guy who makes a crack gets busted right in the kisser."

"Fine," Jerry said. "We'll have to take it outside and load the receiver and batteries in it. The loop can sit right on top of the set, and I've got my flashlight so we can watch the S-meter as we turn the loop. First, though, let's install the transmitter on Bosco."

This was easily and simply done by firmly taping the little transmitter case to the top straps of Bosco's harness that had been put on him for the occasion. The dog promptly gave the transmitter a shakedown test by rolling over and over and trying in vain to scratch it loose with his hind paws. Then apparently satisfied the transistor transmitter could "take it," he proceeded to ignore its presence completely.

By the time the boys were called for supper, the receiver had been installed in the baby buggy and tested. It worked to perfection. Whenever the plane of the shielded loop was at right angles to Bosco, the signal indication from the transmitter on the communication receiver's S-meter fell to zero; but as soon as the loop was rotated slightly on its vertical axis, the meter reading started up and reached a broad maximum as the plane of the loop became parallel to a line drawn to it from the transmitter's location. By using the sharp null reception position as a pointer, the shifting direction of the dog as he

gambolled about the yard could be easily followed; furthermore, the intensity of the received signal gave a rough idea of the animal's distance from the receiver.

Bosco was chained to the clothes line to prevent his taking off while the boys were eating, but as soon as they had bolted their meals they unfastened him and waited impatiently for him to start his mysterious journey. Perversely, though, he seemed to be in no hurry as he casually disinterred a couple of buried bones for critical inspection and then curled up under the perambulator for a short nap. Finally, though, he crawled out from beneath the baby buggy, stretched luxuriously, and then trotted purposefully out the gate into the alley.

"There he goes," Carl whispered excitedly. "He's got that faraway look in his eyes that he always has just before he starts."

"Well, don't just stand there; let's get going!" Jerry exclaimed as both boys grabbed the broad handle of the baby buggy and started off in rattling pursuit of the dog. For a short distance Bosco trotted straight down the middle of the alley, but then he stopped and looked questioningly at the two boys who had also stopped a half block behind him. Then the animal abruptly dived through a hole in a board fence at the side of the alley and disappeared from view.

"He's starting evasive action," Jerry exclaimed as they hurried to the spot where the dog had last been seen. Stopping here, Jerry began swinging the loop back and forth as Carl held the flashlight on the S-meter of the receiver.

"Contact!" Jerry announced dramatically. "He's moving parallel to the alley, but he's staying in the back yards to our left. Now he's cutting back to the alley. Can you see him?"

"There he is," Carl announced. "He's back in the alley but a whole block away. Let's take after him!"

The boys took off in hot pursuit, and immediately Bosco faded back into the shadows on the right side of the alley this time. His attempt to shake off his pursuers did him no good, though, for whenever they stopped they could spot his direction as easily as if they could see him. Fortunately his zig-zag course kept on in the general direction of the alley, and from time to time the boys would get a glimpse of him in the distance by the light of an alley lamp. These glimpses and the weakening indication on the S-meter soon revealed that Bosco, in spite of his circuitous course, was making much better time than the perambulator.

"At this rate," Jerry announced breathlessly, "he's going to get beyond the reach of that little transmitter soon. It's having to stop to take a reading that slows us down. Hm-m-m-m. I do believe there is room for me in the back of that buggy, if you think you can push me. That way I could keep a continuous check on him as we went along and we could soon catch up, but—"

"Get in, get in!" Carl commanded. "The way you're puffing, you'd not last more than a block or so anyway; and while you're yakking, that uranium mine is slipping through our fingers."

Jerry promptly clambered into the back of the buggy. Before handing him the flashlight, Carl couldn't resist bending over to tickle his chum beneath his round chin as he said in syrupy tones, "Kitchee, kitchee, coo; whose little baby are you?" Then he jumped back just in time to avoid being kicked violently in the stomach by Jerry's fast-moving foot.

With the new arrangement the boys rapidly closed the gap between them and Bosco. While Carl pantingly propelled his strange cargo over the rough bricks of the alley, Jerry kept up a continuous patter of: "He's about thirty degrees off the starboard bow—now he's stopped—there he goes again—whoa, slow down; we've gone past him—okay, lift the anchor; he's starting forward."

So intent were the boys on the pursuit that before they realized it they were almost a mile from home, and the houses were beginning to thin out.

"Hey," Jerry suddenly announced over his shoulder, "he's heading for the city dump."

"Good," Carl muttered darkly. "I know something I'd like to dump right now."

It was not difficult to follow the dog along the winding paths through the rubbish left open for the dump trucks, and finally Jerry announced that Bosco had stopped moving just a short distance to the right of the path. Carl stopped the perambulator, and Jerry turned the flashlight on the miniature cliff of ashes, tin cans, and paper boxes that rose in that direction. Suddenly revealed in the bright circle of light stood Bosco, but he was not alone. Standing at his shoulder was a smooth-haired little brown dog of uncertain ancestry, and around their feet played two roly-poly little puppies.

"Well, whaddaya know!" Carl said softly; "Old Bosco is a family man."

"No doubt about that," Jerry agreed as he climbed out of the creaking perambulator, "and that explains why Bosco takes off every evening, but it still does not explain where he picks up the radiation. Bring along your detecting gizmo, and let's climb up there."

In a moment the two boys were squatted at the mouth of the shallow little cave in which Bosco's wife and children had been living—and the radiation detector was clicking away in rising excitement.

"The hot spot is right here in front of the den," Carl announced as he moved the detector back and forth. Reaching down he brushed away the dirt at that point and quickly came to four or five pieces of thin metal about three inches square. As he picked up one of these and held it close to the detector, the clicking rose to a crescendo.

"Pure plates of uranium," Carl said with wide eyes.

"Turn over that 'pure plate,'" Jerry suggested with a grin.

As Carl obeyed, he gasped in surprise and then began to chuckle.

"Discarded clock faces with fluorescent numbers," he exclaimed. "They doubtless are rejects from that alarm clock factory on the other side of town. Bosco has been getting a little of the fluorescent material on his feet whenever he called on his family, and then the stuff gave my radiation detector fits until it wore off. Oh well, I never wanted to be rich anyway."

"Me neither," Jerry said as he fondled one of the cuddly little puppies, "but what are we going to do with Bosco's family? We can't leave them here."

"And why should we when we have a carriage awaiting that was built especially for twins?" Carl waved at the perambulator down below.

In a few minutes the mother dog and her two offspring were comfortably bedded down in the perambulator, and the boys were pushing it along toward home. Overhead a bright moon smiled down on them and on Bosco trotting proudly ahead and glaring fiercely into the shadows for any lurking dangers that might threaten the group under his protection.

"This has been fun," Carl announced contentedly. "There's something about solving a mystery that makes you feel good."

"Yes," Jerry agreed, "and the thing I like is that our electronic apparatus worked so well. If there *had* been a uranium deposit, we'd have found it just as easily as we found those clock faces. Guess we can chalk up a victory for Electronic Experimenters, Ltd."   —30—

OPERATION STARTLED STARLING

Jerry Bishop was in his basement laboratory busily trying to get the sound effect of a horse plodding through deep mud down on the tape of a new recorder he had received for Christmas. He was so engrossed in plopping a couple of his mother's cookie cutters up and down in a shallow dish filled with water near the recorder microphone that he scarcely looked up when the outside door was kicked open and Carl Anderson, his neighbor and best friend, strode in carrying a bird cage held gingerly out in front of him.

"The next time you get a bright idea, Buster, you can do some of the legwork yourself," Carl growled as he set the cage down on the workbench.

"Ah, you got one!" Jerry exclaimed as he shut off the recorder and strolled over to examine the medium-sized black bird with beady eyes and rather ruffled plumage inside the cage. "He doesn't look like he's hurt a bit. How did you ever catch him?"

"It wasn't easy. Some men were shooting the starlings with shotguns around the courthouse, and that little buzzard had the ends of the feathers on one wing shot off. That didn't hurt him any, but it sure messed up his flying. At that, I had to chase him a couple of blocks before I caught him, and he managed to chew about thirty cents worth of hide off the back of my hand while I was stuffing him into the cage. Believe me, Old Scissorbill here is a crazy, mixed-up starling; he thinks he's an eagle or some other kind of meat-eating bird."

"He does have a kind of nasty expression on his face," Jerry agreed as he looked at the bird glaring defiantly up at him.

"This whole idea sounds strictly for the birds to me," Carl blurted out. "Tell it to me again. Maybe it will sound better if I hear it once more."

"Last winter," Jerry patiently related, "a couple of zoologists at Penn State College captured a live starling and made a tape recording of its cries of distress. Then the recorder was installed in a truck equipped with a public address system parked beneath some trees infested with an estimated 20,000 starlings. After the birds were settled for the night, the recording, tremendously amplified, was played through the public address speakers. The birds awakened to the distressed screams of one of their fellows, fled in terror, and never returned. We are going to try to work the same thing on the starlings roosting in the trees in the back yard."

"Still sounds wacky," Carl commented; "but let's get on with it. You hold Scissorbill, and I'll work the recorder."

"Now wait a minute," Jerry said hastily. "You'd better hold the bird and let me operate the recorder. After all, you two are already acquainted. On top of that, this is a pretty critical recording, and everything has to be just right. The tape must be run at the right speed; the gain control must be set just so; the—"

"Oh, all right," Carl said resignedly. "I didn't really expect to get away with it, but it was worth a try. What do you mean the tape has to run at the right speed?"

"To make the bird's cries sound natural, we must have good high-frequency response. That means the tape will need to be run at its top speed of 7½ inches per second."

"How come higher tape speed improves the high frequency response?"

"The recording head translates a sound wave of a given pitch into pulses of magnetic energy that 'prints' the magnetic coating of the moving tape with regularly spaced areas of magnetism. As the pitch or frequency of the sound goes up, these areas are spaced closer and closer to each other until finally, when the frequency of the sound wave is high enough, they start to merge together and so lose their separate identity that must be maintained if the sound is to be reproduced naturally. Now if we speed up the tape, this increases the separation of these magnetized areas; and we can then increase the frequency of the sound wave considerably before the areas start overlapping again."

While Jerry was talking he had removed the tape reels from the recorder and started a short endless loop of tape running through the recording head. The microphone was placed on the edge of the bench, and Carl cautiously opened the door of the cage and reached inside for the bird.

"Yow!" he yelled as the starling viciously chomped down on his finger.

"Shut up," Jerry callously commanded. "We want the starling's cry of distress, not yours. We don't want to scare people."

Carl gave him a scorching look and then, angered, reached inside the cage and hauled the bird unceremoniously forth. Holding it upside down by its feet, he dangled it near the microphone while it screached and screamed its protest at this treatment.

"That's fine," Jerry said. "Now let's see what we've got."

The recorder was switched to "Play," and instantly the basement was filled with a loud cacaphony of raucous screaming that even seemed to take Old Scissorbill aback. At least he became quiet and listened attentively with his head cocked to one side.

"That certainly ought to do it," Jerry said.

"I don't know," Carl said dubiously. "That bird wasn't scared; he was mad. I'll bet a nickel that instead of calling, 'Help, help!' he was really saying something like, 'Let go of my leg, cuss you!' Can I wring his neck now?"

"Sure, but you won't," Jerry said with a grin on his round face. "You don't fool me. I know how chickenhearted you are."

"Chickenhearted, my eye," Carl said with a fierce scowl. "However, I think I'll just turn him loose and let a cat get him. That will be the kind of fate he deserves. Wringing his neck would be too easy a death."

"Uh huh," Jerry said with a knowing smirk; "but now we've got to arrange a way of putting some real punch behind this recording. I thought we could use that twenty-watt speech amplifier and modulator you use to modulate that command transmitter of your ham station. Let's see, that modulation transformer has a 5000 ohm output, doesn't it?"

"Right."

"And here's the speaker I intended to use," Jerry remarked as he dived into a corner of the basement and pulled forth a large speaker with a bell-shaped trumpet. "I've been hanging on to this for a long time hoping to find a use for it. This job is rated at twenty-five watts and has an eight-ohm voice coil."

"Not a very good match for 5000 ohms," Carl observed.

"That's where this audio transformer will come in—I hope," Jerry said as he lifted a heavy transformer on to the bench. "Someone gave me the thing, but no instruction sheet came with it. The primary terminals are lettered, and the secondary terminals simply are numbered from 1 to 16. However, by looking up this model in a catalogue, I know the transformer is rated at twenty watts, that the primary is tapped for use across either 3000 or 5000 ohms, and that the secondary is designed to feed any voice coil impedance from one to thirty ohms. All we have to do is figure out which primary and secondary taps to use so that our eight-ohm voice coil will be properly matched to the 5000 ohm output of the modulation transformer."

"How are you going to do that?"

"First, let's use the ohmmeter of our volt-ohm-milliammeter to measure the d.c. resistance appearing between the various primary taps. Across terminals P-P we measure 600 ohms, while there is only 500 ohms across P^1-P^1. We may safely assume that the higher D.C. resistance indicates that the entire primary winding, designed for an A.C. impedance of 5000 ohms, is connected between the two terminals marked P."

"That's easy, but how about the secondary taps?"

"Well, we know that the impedance ratio between the primary and secondary of a matching transformer is equal to the square of the turns ratio of these two windings, check?"

"Check."

"Our impedance ratio is equal to 5000/8 or 625/1. The square root of that is—" Jerry settled back on the couch with his battered slide rule, but Carl interrupted with, "Twenty-five to one."

"You're right, you mathematical genius!" Jerry exclaimed as he double-checked with the rule. "We also know that if we put a certain

A.C. voltage into one winding of a transformer and then measure the voltage appearing across the other winding, the ratio between the two voltages is equal to the turns ratio of the two windings. So-o-o-o, all we have to do is put twenty-five volts into the primary winding and then measure the voltages appearing between the various taps of the secondary until we find a pair producing quite close to one volt. When these two taps are found, we can connect our eight-ohm voice coil to them and be sure that when the whole primary is connected to the output of the modulation transformer, we'll have a complete match all the way around, which will insure a maximum transfer of power with a minimum of distortion."

"Well, let's quit yakking and get with it," Carl, the man of action, said impatiently.

"Okay. This war-surplus filament transformer puts out almost exactly twenty-five volts of A.C., so connect it to the primary of the transformer, and we'll start measuring. the voltages; across the secondary taps."

In a matter of minutes the boys located a pair of secondary taps that indicates precisely one volt on the A.C. scale of their volt-ohmmeter. The ends of a heavy fifty-foot extension cord were soldered to them, and the other ends of this cord were fastened to the speaker terminals. The primary of the matching transformer was connected to the secondary of the modulation transformer of Carl's amateur station speech equipment. A phone plug with a six-ohm, one-watt resistor fastened across its terminals was plugged in the "External Speaker" jack of the recorder, and a shielded lead went from the two ends of this resistor to the high-level input jack of the speech amplifier. The six-ohm resistor furnished a proper load for the secondary of the recorder's output transformer when the unit's six-ohm speaker voice coil was automatically disconnected by plugging into the jack.

By the time this rather weird lashup of equipment was completed, the boys had already received the third supper call; so they decided to suspend operations until after the evening meal. Right after supper, though, Carl was back over wearing a bright yellow slicker.

"There's a pretty good drizzle going," he announced.

"It takes a pretty mean guy to try and scare a poor little starling out of his nice warm tree on a night like this," Jerry said teasingly.

"Yeah!" Carl snarled as he' rubbed his sore finger and made a threatening gesture at Old Scissorbill, still resting in his cage;

"I can hardly wait."

"Okay. You get outside the basement window, and I'll hand the speaker out to you. That way our cord will allow us to get right under the tree with the speaker. I want to be out there too when the fun starts, so I'm going to get everything down here going but the tape recorder. Then I'll turn it on and dash out there with you while the recorder amplifier is warming up."

This plan was put into action. Jerry switched on the recorder, flipped the volume control well over to the "loud" side of its rotation, took a quick look to make sure the loop of tape was going smoothly past the playback head, and then dashed out the basement door, slamming it shut behind him. It was so dark in the back yard that he stumbled into Carl before he was able to make out the yellow-coated figure of his friend standing there in the cold drizzle expectantly pointing the open mouth of the loudspeaker straight up into the tree branches overhead.

For what seemed an interminably long time, nothing at all was heard from the speaker; but then a beginning murmur of sound quickly swelled into a screaming roar. Just as a photographic enlargement of some small, familiar object converts it into a grotesque, unrecognizable thing, so did the great amplification of the starling's screeching change the sound into a hoarse, brazen noise totally unlike anything either of the awestruck boys had ever heard before. The thought flitted through Jerry's mind that a dinosaur in his death throes must have made a sound like this. Porch lights flashed on up and down the street, and shafts of light streamed across back yards as rear doors were thrown open.

"Shut it off! Quick!" Carl screamed directly into Jerry's ear.

Released from his trance by this suggestion, Jerry turned and in a stumbling run clattered down the basement steps and threw his weight against the door. It did not budge. The night latch on the inside had locked itself. Hesitating only a minute, Jerry bounded back up the steps with a vigor most unusual to his leisure-loving nature and ran around to the front of the house, through the front door, down the

hall, down the basement steps, and into his laboratory. He made a flying leap across the room, and his clawing fingers switched off the tape recorder.

Instantly the bellowing stopped, only to be followed by shouting and the sound of running feet going past the basement windows. Jerry turned off the basement light and stood there panting in the darkness for a few seconds until he could regain his breath; then he very quietly opened the outside basement door and tiptoed up the steps.

The back yard was no longer in darkness. Carl was sitting squarely in the center of a blinding circle of light cast by the spotlight of a police squadcar parked in the alley; and two policemen, who seemed unnecessarily large, were getting out of the car. Neighbors carrying flashlights were flitting around like fireflies.

"All right, all right," one of the policemen said, "which one of you called in that report about a dog being run over in this alley?"

"Yeah," his fellow officer chimed in, "and which one reported there was a panther ten feet long slinking up and down and screaming its head off back here? Was it you?" he demanded of Carl.

"No sir," Carl promptly replied. "I heard an awful noise, but I didn't see a panther or hear any dog."

For a few minutes the policemen questioned the neighbors without getting any two of them to agree on what the noise sounded like. Then they flashed the spotlight all around, peered into a few garages and basement entrances, and finally decided the whole thing was a false alarm.

"Probably some guy with a stuck automobile horn caused all this hullabaloo," one of them remarked as he got back into the squad car. "Sonny, you had better get into the house out of this drizzle," he advised Carl as they started to drive away.

"Yessir," Carl said meekly without moving.

Jerry sidled out to Carl and asked out of the corner of his mouth, "Where the heck is the speaker?"

"What do you think I'm sitting on?" Carl demanded in a hoarse whisper as he spread out the tail of his overcoat a little more. "I was scared to death they'd trip over the cord, but they never even saw it."

In a few minutes the neighbors drifted away, and the boys got the speaker back inside the basement.

"We'll not try that again," Jerry said emphatically; "and the heck of it is I was too excited to notice if we scared any starlings or not."

"I wasn't," Carl answered. "While the cops were playing their spotlight and flashlights around, I kept looking up in the tree. The birds did take off at first, but they just made a little circle and came right back as soon as the noise stopped."

"Those Penn State starlings must be a timid, cowardly crew totally unrelated to Old Scissorbill and his hardboiled chums," Jerry offered.

"Nope," Carl demurred, "I still think that pint-sized eagle crossed us up. During that hour or so while you were leisurely shutting off the recorder, I had to listen to that racket coming right up in my face, and I'll swear that what Old Scissorbill was yelling didn't sound like 'Take to the hills!' at all; instead, it sounded more like, 'Hey, Rube! Come and help me take 'em!' "

"Well," Jerry remarked as he prepared to turn out the lights, "I guess Electronic Experimenters, Ltd., will have to chalk this up as a howling failure—but it had its moments!"   ⎯30⎯

TWO DETECTORS

February 1955

At Jerry's invitation, Carl had accompanied him to Carter's Feed Store on their way home from school. Not until they were inside the store did the long and rangy Carl learn that his chubby companion had a reason behind his invitation: he wanted help in carrying home some of his recording equipment that was at the store. Jerry thanked Mr. Carter profusely for something—Carl could not make out exactly for what—and the two boys started home. By some chance Carl found himself carrying the tape recorder that weighed a good thirty pounds, while Jerry padded along carrying a timer clock whose weight could be measured in ounces.

"You know," Carl ruminated aloud, "I used to wonder why you didn't take up with a good strong packhorse for a chum instead of me; but then I realized you would have to feed a horse!"

"Let's not be bitter!" Jerry said as he delicately steadied the clock on top of his flat-top crewcut with the right forefinger while, with his left hand on his hip, he minced along with the exaggerated prance of a baton twirler beside the trudging Carl. "You are a victim of what might be called *muscle oblige,* which is French for, "Them as has muscles has gotta use 'em.'"

"That's so nice to know," Carl observed sarcastically. "Why did you have this recording junk down at the feedstore, anyway?"

"I wanted to make a recording of rats squealing, and that store has got the rats. I nailed a piece of meat to the floor just under the microphone and set this timer clock to cut the recorder on for fifteen minutes around midnight. I figured that by that time the rats would be

41

having a real ball and I ought to get some dandy squealing."

"And why," Carl patiently pursued, "did you want a recording of rats squealing?"

"For the new party game tape I'm working out called *Horror Story Sound Effects*. On this tape will be several sound effect strips, each one representing the sounds that might have been heard in an important scene from a well-known horror story. At a party this tape will be played in the darkness and the guests will try to guess the title of the story represented by each sound effect. As an example, I rasp a mason's trowel across a brick a few times, rattle a chain, and give a muffled crazy laugh with the microphone shut up in my clothes closet. That represents the scene where Fortunate is being walled up in *The Cask of Amontillado,* by Poe."

"Hey, that's keen," Carl applauded.

"For *The Pit and the Pendulum,* I want to use the sound effect for the story's climax where the swinging crescent of sharp steel is just about to cut into the victim while the rats are squealing and fighting as they gnaw at his food-smeared bonds. Swishing a wood lath back and forth in front of the microphone takes care of the sound of the swinging knife, but nothing quite sounds like a rat squealing but a rat himself."

"Well," Carl observed as they reached the basement entrance of Jerry's laboratory, "We'll soon know what we've got on the tape."

In a few minutes the recorder was set up and the boys were listening intently to the faint rustling sounds coming from the speaker. At first, these were the only sounds heard, but after a few minutes the rats apparently became accustomed to the slight noise made by the running recorder and returned to their feast. As they did so, their fighting and squealing rose to a crescendo, which was all Jerry could want. He reached over to switch off the recorder, but just as he did so a sound came from the speaker that stopped his hand in midair. It was a man's gruff voice, faint and muffled, but clearly understandable:

"You're late. How come?"

"The job took longer than I expected," a younger man's voice replied. "She took an awful lot of choking before she finally died and I had to drag her into the garage."

"No one saw or heard you, did they? Those Hollywood types get a lot of attention."

"I'm sure they didn't. Now I've got another problem. The boss says I've got to get rid of the body right away. How about your helping me dump it tomorrow night?"

"Okay. Do you think we ought to cut it up first to make identification impossible?"

"That won't be necessary. We can just throw the body on your flatbed truck and spread a canvas over it and then drive to that old abandoned stone quarry west of town. Once it's at the bottom of that, no one is ever going to find it."

"All right, I'll be over at your place with the truck about twelve-thirty tomorrow night; then we can—"

At this point the slapping of a freed end announced that the short tape had passed through the machine.

"Holy cow!" Carl breathed softly, "What a time to run out of tape! We've been listening to a couple of murderers!"

"And the victim must have been a pretty Hollywood starlet," Jerry said, his staring round eyes matching his round face. "That microphone was hanging just below a window that opens out into an alley. Those killers must have been standing just outside that window."

"Well, what are we waiting for?" Carl demanded as he jumped to his feet. "Let's take this recording down to the police."

"Hold on," Jerry admonished. "Don't forget that since the police found we were behind that starling-scaring business, we are not exactly the fair-haired boys with them. If we take this down there now, they will think we cooked the whole thing up ourselves."

"Surely you're not going to just sit there and let those crooks get away with choking that pretty little starlet to death, are you?" Carl demanded as he paced impatiently up and down the laboratory.

"No, but we've got to go at this calmly," Jerry announced as he assumed his favorite position on the couch with his head pillowed on his clasped hands. "After all, the crime has already been committed, so we can't stop it from happening. What we want to do is make sure the murderers are punished, right?"

"I guess so."

"We know they are going to try and dispose of the body tonight shortly after midnight; and we are both familiar with the quarry where this is to take place. All we have to do is let them try to carry out their plan and then arrange for the police to catch them right in the act."

"And just how, if I may be so bold as to ask, are we going to manage this little thing?"

"Suppose tonight we ride our bicycles out to the west edge of town and take along a couple of those two-meter walkie-talkies our radio club built up for Civilian Defense work. One of us can station himself at the stone quarry, and the other can stay close to that all-night drugstore at the edge of town. That means we'll only be about a mile apart and can communicate with each other easily. Then when you— I mean when the person at the quarry sees the truck turning into the quarry gate he can flash the word to the fellow at the drugstore. This fellow can then telephone the police to send a squad car to the stone quarry. After the squad car has arrived and caught the cold-blooded killers right in the act of disposing of the body, we can come forward and modestly admit we were the detectors—I mean the detectives— who engineered the whole clever affair. Any questions?"

"Just one," Carl said slowly as he glowered suspiciously down at the reclining figure of his chum. "Who stands watch at the quarry?"

"Why, Carl," Jerry said with round-eyed elaborate carelessness, "I hadn't even thought about that, but I'd better take the job. Of course, since I'm short-legged and a little inclined to be pleasingly plump, I couldn't run very fast if something went wrong, and the men would be sure to catch me and send me down to the bottom of the quarry too, but that's all the more reason why I wouldn't want my best friend to take any chances, even though he is the fastest sprinter our high school has ever had. After all—"

"All right, all right!" Carl interrupted. "I'll go to the quarry; but don't think you suckered me into it. It's just that I'd as soon be scared to death as talked to death. I'll get the gear together and see you back in the alley about eleven o'clock."

But Carl did not get out of the house at eleven. His folks were watching the late TV show, and it was impossible for him to get out of the house without their noticing until almost a quarter to twelve. The two boys rode their bicycles swiftly to the edge of town and there they parted. Jerry took up his vigil in a dark shadow beside the drugstore, while Carl bravely rode off into the darkness along the road leading past the quarry.

It seemed a long time before Jerry suddenly heard Carl's welcome voice in the earphone of the walkie-talkie pressed close against his ear: "W9CFI, this is W9EGV calling. How do you copy?"

"Five by nine," Jerry said softly with his lips almost touching the mike of the transceiver. "Where are you?"

"Under the bridge that leads off the road into the quarry," Carl reported. "This ditch is dry and deep enough for me and my bike both to get under here. What time is it?"

Jerry cautiously peered around the corner of the building at the clock hanging in the front window before he announced, "Twelve forty-five. See anything of the murderers yet?"

"Don't use that word!" Carl said hoarsely. "I hope this doesn't take long. It's not exactly cozy under this bridge."

"I believe that," Jerry said, "because I can, hear your teeth chattering."

"Hey, I see a pair of lights coming down the road," Carl announced excitedly. "I'm going to duck back under the bridge, and if you hear the truck pass over, get ready to make that phone call *muy pronto*. It's getting closer; now it's slowing down—" his voice trailed off at this point, but he kept the transmit switch held down, and Jerry could distinctly hear the hollow rumble as a heavy vehicle passed over the wooden bridge.

"It's them," Carl said in a hoarse whisper with a reckless disregard for his English. "Make that call and ride out here as fast as your fat little legs will carry you. I may need help."

Waiting to hear no more, Jerry tossed the transceiver into the basket of his bicycle and slipped into the phone booth of the drugstore. He dialed the already-memorized police number and tucked his chin down so as to make his voice come from his chest,

rendering it— he hoped—deeper and more mature. As soon as a man's voice answered, he carefully intoned: "Listen carefully. Two murderers are disposing of the body of a victim at this very moment at the old stone quarry a mile west of town. If you send a squad car immediately, you can catch them in the act."

Then, without waiting for an answer, he quietly hung up the receiver and slid out of the drugstore. Now, ordinarily Jerry had an almost pathological aversion to exercise in any form, but let it be said to his credit that this once he did not spare the horsepower as he pedaled swiftly down the road toward his friend in danger. The night was dark, and he kept his bicycle light turned off. This made it very difficult to tell exactly where he was, especially since his eyes were still not completely accustomed to the darkness. Just as he was thinking that he must be nearing the quarry, there was a sudden pinging sound. His bicycle rose beneath him like a bucking bronco, and he sailed over the handlebars to make a perfect three-point landing on his knees and nose in the frozen gravel of the roadway.

Before he could gather his scattered senses, Carl was dragging him by an elbow toward the deep ditch at the side of the road and hissing into his ear, "Get down here in the ditch before they see us. I crawled up a few yards to wait for you, but you came along so fast I didn't have time to flag you down. I was afraid to call out, so I just grabbed up a stick and ran it through your front spokes. That stopped you!"

"Oh fine!" Jerry muttered as he tenderly felt his scraped nose. "Here I am rushing to help you, and you try to murder me."

"Quit griping," Carl hissed. "With all that natural padding you've got, a little bump isn't going to do any damage. Let's get back under the bridge until the squad car comes."

They had barely reached this sanctuary before they heard the wailing of a police siren, and a few seconds later the flashing red light of a squad car rapidly approached down the road. With a great screeching of brakes and showering of gravel the car slowed down and turned abruptly across the bridge. The boys immediately popped out of their hiding place to see a truck and two men standing in the glare of the squad-car spotlights.

"All right, you two; don't move!" one of the officers commanded as he stepped from the car with a drawn gun. "What are you up to?"

"Why we were just getting ready to dump a body—" one of the men began.

"Ha! So you admit it," the officer said menacingly. "Mack, you cover me while I examine the body."

With his gun still drawn, the policeman stepped forward cautiously, taking care not to come between the gun of his fellow officer and the two men, and jerked the canvas from the object on the truck. The two boys had stolen out of the ditch and were standing right at the rear fender of the squad car. The simultaneous gasp they gave as the canvas slipped to the ground so unnerved the policeman standing beside the car that he tried to point his gun in all four directions at the same time and came very close to shooting a hole in the squad car itself.

"It's a car body!" the boys said in chorus.

"And what did you think it was?" demanded one of the men in the spotlight.

"Hey, where did you kids come from? Did one of you call us?" the officer near the car demanded.

"Ye-yes, I did," Jerry quavered. Then he told the whole story of the tape recording. Before he finished the two men with the truck were slapping each other on the back and laughing so hard they could scarcely stand up. Finally the younger one wiped his eyes and started to explain:

"I do some dirt track racing. Jack here, who works at a machine shop from 4 p.m. until midnight, helps me fix up my cars. I often talk with him after he eats a midnight snack at the restaurant right across the alley from the feed store. Last night I was telling him about a beat-up racecar I had bought in a neighboring town and had managed to drive home. The heap was in such sad shape that I had to keep choking the motor to make it run. It finally died completely right in front of the house and I had to tow it into my garage. We were't going to use the old body and my wife said I had to get rid of it. I call my wife 'The Boss'—just kidding, of course."

"We're both married; we understand," one of the policemen said.

"In this race business, every driver likes to keep the other drivers guessing about a new rod he intends to use. That's why we didn't want anyone to see the car we were rebuilding. Leaving the old body lying around would be a giveaway, so we were going to drop it into the quarry."

"What was that about 'the Hollywood type attracting a lot of attention,'" Carl asked.

"The jalop had a Hollywood muffler on it that made a lot of noise when you gunned the motor," Jack explained promptly.

The older policeman studied the dejected faces of the two boys for a few seconds and then said kindly, "Don't take it so hard, fellows. Even without hearing that tape, I can imagine how convincing it must have sounded. And if it *had* been a serious affair, you did a good job of detecting."

Jerry looked up with a sudden expression of resolution. "From now on," he announced, " 'detection' is going to be just a radio term as far as I am concerned."

"I'm with you," Carl said fervently as he started toward his bicycle.

—30—

GOING UP, UP, UP

March 1955

It was one of those unseasonably warm days that March often borrows from May and then pays back with a chilly day of its own during the latter month. Jerry Bishop was a victim of this nice weather. Instead of lolling comfortably on the leather-covered couch in his basement laboratory while his nimble mind toyed with some fascinating electronic problem, he found himself standing in the middle of a vast expanse of winter-littered front yard with a rake firmly grasped in his plump hands. Recalling the dark threats his father had made about what would happen if he came home that evening and discovered a single unraked square foot of that yard, the boy plied the rake vigorously.

As he engaged in this unaccustomed and—to his mind—unseemly exercise, Jerry reflected bitterly that at any other time his pal and neighbor, Carl Anderson, would be around to provide Jerry with at least a fifty-fifty chance of inveigling his friend into helping; but Carl had not shown up all day. Like most jobs, though, once started it was not so bad. He had the yard more than half finished an hour later when Carl came dashing around the house with his dog, Bosco, in playful pursuit. Around and around the yard the boy and dog romped while Jerry leaned on his rake handle and looked at this reckless waste of energy with mild disapproval. Finally Carl threw himself on his back at full length in front of Jerry and let Bosco tug and worry at his pants leg while he looked up with a grin and said, "Well, Blubber Boy, how do you like doing a little physical labor for a change? I've been sitting up there with old Mr. Gruber in his room for the past hour watching you. It was an interesting study in slow motion."

"What were you talking to him about?" Jerry asked, ignoring the other remarks.

"I was *trying* to get him to tell me about his experiences with the Rough Riders. I always thought old people enjoyed talking about the past. Well, someone ought to explain this to Mr. Gruber. All he wants to talk about is flying saucers!"

"What about flying saucers?"

"He's read everything about 'em he can get hold of, and he has a stack of science fiction magazines this high," Carl said as he suddenly elevated one powerful, lanky leg straight up in the air to show the height of the magazine stack, with Bosco, his eyes tightly shut, still clinging doggedly to the pants cuff. "Mr. Gruber's convinced the saucers contain people from Mars who are trying to raid the earth, and he keeps a loaded double-barreled shotgun right by his bed to repel an invasion by day or night."

As Carl talked, Jerry walked slowly over to a silvered-ball lawn ornament and stared at it fixedly as he walked around it.

"Crystal gazing will get you nowhere," Carl jeered unsympathetically. "You may as well make with the rake, Jake."

"I was just noticing I could see you and Bosco reflected in this globe, no matter where you were playing with him," Jerry said with a thoughtful look on his round face.

"A fascinating bit of useless information," Carl remarked as he sat up and vigorously wiped his horn-rimmed glasses with a questionable-looking handkerchief.

"No information is useless," Jerry declared reprovingly. "This gives me an idea. TV signals move in straight lines much the same way light does. If we had a silvered ball like this mounted away up in the air where it would be in the direct line-of-sight of signals arriving from the station on Channel 6, sixty-five miles away, those signals would strike different points on the ball and be reflected down into every location in town, where TV antennas pointed right at the ball should provide excellent reception. A balloon with a metallic painted surface doubtless would serve just as well as the silvered ball. Even if such a spherical balloon moved around, there would always be some point on its surface that would serve to reflect the signals down to a given antenna, just as there was always a point on this ball that reflected the light waves from you and Bosco to my eye."

"Well, since we don't have a balloon—" Carl suddenly stopped short and clapped a hand over his mouth.

"Hey! You know where there *is* a balloon!" Jerry accused excitedly.

"Me and my big mouth!" Carl exclaimed in disgust. "I just remembered that I have a rubber balloon six feet in diameter and a cylinder of compressed helium to inflate it. Dad picked them up at a war surplus store some time ago. I'm saving the balloon for amateur Field Day. Then I'm going to see how our portable club station transmitter can get out with a long wire vertical antenna."

"Aw, c'mon, Carl, you don't want to wait until then to try out your balloon," Jerry wheedled. "Maybe that cylinder has enough helium in it to fill the balloon several times. Let's spray it with a coat of aluminum paint and see how my idea works tonight."

"We-1-1-1, I dunno," Carl said slowly, obviously weakening. "How high would it have to go, and what would we use to hold it? I was going to use wire out in the country, of course."

"Using wire on a balloon in town, around all the wires carrying high voltage electricity, would be about as healthy as rubbing noses with a cobra," Jerry observed. "I've got a roll of binder twine in the basement that'll be just the stuff. As to how high we've got to go, let's see now . . ." He pulled a battered slide rule from his hip pocket and began working with it as he talked.

"I remember the formula for determining how far out you can see on the earth's surface from a high point, allowing only for the normal curvature of the earth. $D = 1.23$ times the square root of H_t, where D is the distance you can see in miles and H_t is the height of the viewing position—in this case the top of the transmitting antenna—in feet. Channel 6's tower is just about 1,000 feet; so we take the square root of that, which looks like 31.6, multiply it by 1.23, and we get very, very close to 39 miles.

"Now we know the station is 65 miles away, and 39 from 65 leaves 26 miles as the distance our balloon must be able to 'see' if it is to establish what hams call 'eyeball contact' with the transmitting antenna. Substituting this in our formula gives us 26 = 1.23 times the square root of H_b, where H_b is the needed height of the balloon in feet. Dividing both sides of the equation by 1.23 gives us about 21.1 = H_b. Squaring both sides of this yields 445 = H_b. In other words, our balloon should be around 450 feet in the air for line-of-sight reception. In actual practice, the height worked out by this formula can be decreased by a factor of from 1.25 to 1.35 to allow for the refraction that TV signals experience in the earth's atmosphere that ordinarily increase the 'virtual line-of-sight' distances beyond the true line-of-sight figures. Just to be safe, though, I think we'll stick to the figure worked out."

"Well, let's get going," Carl said as he sprang to his feet and vigorously brushed off the seat of his trousers.

"I'd like to," Jerry said wistfully, "but I've got to finish this yard first. Of course, if you were to get your rake and help. . . ."

"All right, all *right!*" Carl shouted over his shoulder as he hurdled the fence between his yard and Jerry's. "I might have known I'd be suckered into something if I came around while you had work to do, but maybe this will teach me a lesson. I'll be right back with the rake."

He was as good as his word, and the remainder of the yard was quickly finished. Carl's explosive energy made short work of the leaves and twigs—and even of some of the grass roots! As soon as the yard was done, both boys tossed their rakes aside and made a beeline for Carl's garage. There Carl fished a long box out of an old trunk and opened it to reveal the limp carcass of a large yellow rubber balloon and a small metal cylinder of gas. It took only minutes to attach the two and open the valve. There was a great hissing sound, and the wrinkled envelope swelled and smoothed out into a beautiful golden sphere. Apparently the man who filled the cylinder calculated very nicely, for just as the balloon reached a diameter of roughly six feet, the hissing noise stopped and the rubber sphere ceased to grow.

"'Maybe the cylinder has enough helium in it to fill the balloon several times,' he says," Carl quoted bitterly.

"So I was wrong," Jerry cheerfully admitted as he closed the valve in the neck of the balloon. "Wups!" he exclaimed as the neck slipped from his fingers and the balloon soared up and bumped along the rafters of the tall barn that had been converted into a garage. "It's a good thing we didn't fill it out of doors. You get a ladder and recapture the slippery thing while I get our spray gun and put some aluminum paint in it."

Neither operation took long. Carl held the captive balloon and turned it about while Jerry stood on a stepladder and sprayed the surface with metallic paint. Jerry directed the paint spray with more enthusiasm than accuracy, and by the time the job was finished, Carl's face had a metallic sheen that matched the silvery sphere he was holding.

"I'll bet my face cracks six ways the next time I smile," he muttered through stiff lips. "Now I know how the man in the iron mask must have felt. Say, wait a minute!" he exclaimed as he picked up a piece of black tissue paper and began whacking away at it with the tin snips. In a couple of minutes he climbed up on the ladder and pressed the bits of paper against the sticky surface of the balloon. Those bits of paper (serving as eyes, mouth, and nose), transformed the silvery bubble into the bald head of a menacing, snaggle-toothed ogre.

"Holy cow!" Jerry exclaimed, "I'd hate to meet that guy in the dark."

"When I was in the third grade, I won a prize for carving the meanest-looking Halloween pumpkin," Carl modestly admitted.

The boys spent the remaining daylight hours rigging up an old yagi Channel 6 antenna the Bishops had taken down when they had put up their new all-channel antenna and rotor. The yagi was mounted on a broom handle thrust through the rungs of a stepladder so it could be rotated on a horizontal axis.

"By keeping the side of the yagi pointed at the station while the front of it points up in the sky, we can make sure all the reception we get is reflected from the balloon," Jerry explained. "A yagi picks up practically nothing off the side."

Carl's folks had gone out of town for the weekend; so the two boys had the run of the Anderson home. It was thought best to keep the balloon raising point, the yagi antenna, and the TV receiver all as close together as possible so that information could be easily relayed back and forth between the balloon-and-antenna operator and the TV set observer. To this end a short length of twin lead was run from the TV receiveroutthroughawindowtotheyagisetuponashortladderbetween

the Anderson house and the Gruber home next door. The binder twine was measured off and a knot tied every fifty feet so the height of the balloon could be known. When everything was ready, both boys went over to Jerry's house for supper, leaving the balloon safely hidden inside the closed garage. They did not want to send it up until after dark to avoid attracting attention.

By eight o'clock it was quite dark except for the light of a bright moon just coming over the housetops. Carl and Jerry, armed with flashlights, stealthily conveyed the balloon, tugging and bobbing in the gusty breeze, out of the garage and into the narrow space between the houses.

"Sh-h-h, don't make any noise," Carl whispered as he pointed to the lighted window above their heads on the second floor of the Gruber house. "Grandpa Gruber must be catching up on his science fiction reading, and in spite of his eighty years, he's got plenty good ears."

"Okay; let her go up," Jerry commanded.

"Aye, aye, sir; releasing ballast," Carl whispered as he let the coarse binder twine slide through his fingers.

The released balloon soared aloft like a live thing for about twenty feet, and then it stopped with a jerk.

"What's the matter?" Jerry whispered hoarsely.

"Darned twine is tangled," Carl muttered as he fumbled with knots in the darkness. Above their heads the balloon was caught by a gust of wind and lurched over and bumped against the lighted window pane with a soft whumping sound.

"Holy cow! Let it go, tangle and all," came Jerry's agonized plea.

Carl obeyed, and the balloon started up again; but it was too late. From the lighted room there came a sound that was half a scream of fright and half a Rebel yell.

"Boots and saddles! Prepare to mount! Charge!'" came the muffled shouts of Grandpa Gruber. Then his window was thrown open and a long black tube thrust outside. A moment later an orange tongue of flame licked out of the tube toward the balloon, only to be followed a second later by a second jet of flame. Three reports rang out almost as a single clap of sound, and the balloon evaporated from sight. The binder twine dropped back to earth in a tangle over the heads of both boys.

"I got him! I got the varmint!" Grandpa Gruber cackled at the open window, as doors were thrown open and people came running from all directions. "Look for his carcass down there, but keep an eye peeled for some more of them Martians that may be hanging around. He was thirty feet tall with a head as bald as an egg and as big as a barndoor and the skinniest body you ever did see. I got a real good gander at him while he was peeking in my window, and I'll swear I never saw such a mean-looking countenance outside of a nightmare. Hain't you found his carcass yet? Old Betsy here put two loads of chilled shot right between his nasty eyes; and there ain't a thing on this Earth or any of the rest of the planets that can live after a dose like that."

"All right, folks, stand back; what's going on here?" demanded a policeman as he shouldered his way through the crowd.

"Mr. Gruber up there saw somebody—or some thing—peeping into his window and shot at it," a woman explained.

"Peeping into a second story window!" the policeman scoffed. "Grandpa, you'd better close that window and go on back to bed before you catch a cold. You've been having a nightmare."

"Nightmare my eye, young know-it-all!" Mr. Gruber said tartly. "I tell you I saw a man from Mars, and I let moonlight through his pumpkin head with Old Betsy here. If you can't find the body, like as not his companions have lugged it off in one of their saucer ships. But there's no use trying to explain anything to stupid people who read nothing but the comics."

Saying this, Grandpa Gruber slammed down the window, and a few minutes later the light in his room went out.

Jerry and Carl had very quietly and unobtrusively slipped into the Anderson house as soon as the policeman arrived, but they had not escaped his notice. As he got back into the squad car he said reflectively to his fellow officer, "You know, every time there's some excitement, that tall tow-headed kid with the glasses and the short fat one are right on the spot. I wonder how come."

Inside the Anderson home, Carl and Jerry sat on a couch and grinned at each other rather sheepishly.

"That's the end of my Field Day balloon and your experiment," Carl said slowly, "but I guess neither of us minds too much. It was worth it just to let Grandpa Gruber get a good look at one of his saucer folks. I just hope I've got half his zip and fire when I'm that old."

-30-

THE ATTRACTION OF AMATEUR RADIO

April 1955

Spring fever had infected our heroes! Carl and Jerry were busy getting the lawn furniture out of Jerry's basement and cleaning it. This chore finished, both promptly collapsed into a pair of still damp chairs in the middle of the back yard. The "chur-lik chur-lik" of busy robins filled the air and overhead a bright April sun beat down warmly upon them and induced a delicious, languorous drowsiness.

Jerry sat hunched in his chair with his chubby legs curled beneath him, his hands clasped across his stomach, and with his head slumped forward on his chest so that he resembled a sleeping Buddha. Carl's long legs were stretched out in front of him, and he had slid down in the lawn chair so that only the back of his head, the seat of his pants, and his heels dug into the freshly-green sod were supporting his lanky frame. The sun shone through the lenses of his horn-rimmed glasses upon his tightly closed eyelids and created a beautiful, formless, dark-red void for his languid inspection.

"Hey, Jer," Carl drawled feebly.

"Uh huh," Jerry answered drowsily, without stirring an unnecessary muscle.

"I'm giving an oral theme Monday on 'What I Like About My Hobby.' Want to help me dream up something on ham radio?"

"I reckon you can sound off on all the reasons you can think of, and I'll add any I think you miss."

"Okey-dokey. First off, I like amateur radio because it's a hobby in which you *do* things. It always sounds funny to hear some of the fellows griping about there being nothing to do. You and I can't find time to do half of the things we want to. There are always transmitters and receivers and test equipment to build and try out. There are new antennas to be constructed and put up and tested. New circuits must be tried, and of course there's your amateur station to operate. This last is especially important because half the fun of any hobby is talking it over with other people who are as crazy about it as you are. No matter how lonely your neighborhood is, there are always hundreds of other amateurs ready and eager to talk ham stuff with you whenever you place your transmitter on the air.

"Next, it's an exciting hobby. Every time there's a hurricane, tornado, flood, or other disaster anywhere within  several hundred miles, I can have a front row seat just by listening on my station receiver. What's more, I can often be of real help in relaying messages in and out of the stricken area for other ham stations who are right in the thick of things. But even when there is no emergency, operating a ham station is an exciting and suspense-filled experience. For example, when I pound out a CQ on twenty meters, I never know if I'm going to get an answer from half-way around the world—"

"Or perhaps from your old buddy right next door," Jerry broke in with a chuckle.

"True! But that's part of the fun. It's like fishing. You never know just what you're going to pull out. I like the challenge to skill and muscular coordination needed to handle messages at high code speeds. Your nerves must be just as steady to send good clean code as they are to make a high score in rifle shooting or in tossing free buckets in basketball. Copying a guy who's throwing it at you at thirty words a minute means your mind and muscles have to work together as fast as lightning."

"You're making it sound pretty strenuous." Jerry yawned. "Don't you have any reasons without muscles in them?"

"Sure, my flabby friend. One thing is that it has prestige. Not just any stupe can be a ham simply by deciding he wants to be. That little old ham ticket on the wall says a lot of nice things about the guy who owns it. It testifies he's had the gumption to study the code, theory, and laws until he is capable of operating a complicated radio station. Who says so? Uncle Sam himself, because that license is granted by the FCC after giving a stiff examination that's no push-over, even for people who've spent their whole lives in electronics work. Many state governments, too, show what they think of hams by granting them special auto license plates with their call letters. The armed forces encourage this hobby in every way they can, even by having military stations work directly with the amateurs. They know that their best operators and technicians will come from this group. Red Cross and Civil Defense authorities are always ready to work closely with hams. Every time there's a major disaster, you can be sure the newspapers will carry stories on the wonderful work hams perform in restoring broken communications. A ham is *somebody!*

"Another thing I like about hamming is that it allows me to acquire a lot of pretty complicated technical knowledge with hardly any pain or strain. When you're actually working with electronic equipment, reading interesting magazine articles about it, and talking about it with other guys on the air, it's amazing how much knowledge rubs off on you without your knowing it—knowledge that sticks with you, too. It's one thing to read that a parallel-tuned circuit presents maximum impedance at resonance and something entirely different to see the beautiful way in which a final amplifier's plate current dips as the tank circuit is tuned through resonance."

"Now let's not get sickening about this," Jerry objected. "You're beginning to sound pretty lyrical."

"A dull clod with a slide rule for a soul!" Carl muttered. "Well, the final thing about ham radio that I like is the social side of it. By means of my amateur station I've become acquainted with all sorts of people I'd never have met otherwise. I know doctors, editors, lawyers, band leaders, radio and TV comedians, service technicians, policemen, radio station engineers, plumbers, dentists, school superintendents, and people in just about any other walk of life you'd care to mention. They call me 'Carl,' and I call them by their first names. On the ham bands it's not your age or your money or your fame that counts. All that really matters is the quality of the signal you put out with your transmitter and how good your operating procedure is.

"And," Carl concluded, "it's always mighty comforting to know I can go into any strange city and find ham friends who will welcome me into their 'shacks,' whether it be a converted clothes closet or a spacious, beautifully decorated room in a mansion. A ham has friends wherever he travels."

"That's a pretty good list of reasons you have, *Carlos, amigo mio*" Jerry remarked as he straightened up and stretched luxuriously. "I don't have too much to add, but I might say that while you like ham radio because it gives you something to do, I like it because it gives me something to think about. Trying to understand what goes on inside the transmitter and receiver circuits makes me call on every bit of math and chemistry and physics I've ever studied and causes me to realize that I need to know even more. I'm going to learn more, too; and that's another thing in favor of the hobby. It's sort of a sweet, juicy carrot that tempts the ham along the path leading to a career in electrical or electronic engineering. At the very top of every part of these fields you'll find men who first became interested in their work through the hobby of amateur radio.

"Second, I know my hobby will never be outgrown. It has an equal fascination for all ages. Teen-agers, the middle-aged, and retired people are all represented on the ham bands. Both of us know hams who have been following the hobby for thirty or forty years and are just as enthusiastic about it now as they were when they started. One reason for this, I think, is the fact that the hobby is a live and growing thing. New techniques and equipment are constantly being discovered and put to use. I like to hear the old-timers talk about how they've stuck with their hobby from the time they built their first rotary-gap spark transmitter through self-excited vacuum-tube transmitters, crystal-controlled rigs, the first crude telephone equipment, narrow-band frequency modulated jobs, mobile installations, and now single-sideband suppressed-carrier transmitters. Several hams are actually building and using their own facsimile and television transmitters.

"And I must admit that being a ham does nice things to my ego. Here I am working with tiny electrons that can't be seen, felt, heard, tasted, or smelled; yet these powerful little 'assumptions' hop to my command and will carry my voice halfway around the world. When I try to explain what goes on in my equipment to a non-ham, he looks at me as though I were speaking an unknown foreign tongue. All this makes me feel smart and powerful.

"Another good thing about the hobby is that it's one a whole family can enjoy right at home. More and more husband-and-wife amateur teams are heard on the ham bands these days; and it's not at all unusual to find families in which the parents and all the children hold amateur tickets. When so many present-day forces tend to pull families apart, it is nice to discover a hobby that can draw them closer together."

"Now wait just a little minute!" Carl exploded. "If you think I'm going to stand up in front of that English class and say I'm looking forward to having a silly wife and a bunch of little brats help me work my ham rig, you've got rocks in your head. I'd never live it down. I can just hear those dizzy dames in the class snickering right now."

"All right, all right!" Jerry soothed. "Leave it out, even though it is a good point. Instead, you can sign off with this thought: as we two have just demonstrated, one of the best things about this hobby is that it has so many different appeals. If you like to build things with your hands and watch them work, ham radio is your dish. The fellow who likes to study abstract theory will find an equal fascination here. Using code will appeal to the person who likes to master an exacting skill. If you are the social type and get your kicks out of just yakking with other people, amateur radio is the perfect hobby. The experimenter who loves to try new circuits and techniques will never run out of material in his ham shack. And the person—"

"Hold it!" Carl broke in. "I think I've got the perfect idea to close the talk. You know how hipped Miss Richason, our English teacher, is on the use of quotations. Well, I happened to be glancing through a book on Roman history in the library the other day—this was my Latin teacher's idea; not mine—and I read a couple of paragraphs in which the writer was explaining why that doll, Cleopatra, was able to snow all the guys back in her day. As he saw it, she could do this because her personality had so many different forms. As he put it rather neatly, taking a line from the Bible, she was 'All things to all men.' How's about my saying that this is a perfect description of ham radio? All of us are in love with our hobby and never grow tired of it because it is 'All things to all men.' "

"Perfect!" Jerry applauded. "If that doesn't wangle an 'A' for you, I'll eat my log book. And now we've talked about ham radio so much that I'm beginning to feel a nasty surge of ambition. What say we go down into the basement and put in a few licks on that two-meter rig of mine?"

"I'm with you," Carl exclaimed as he jumped to his feet. "Let's go!"

—30—

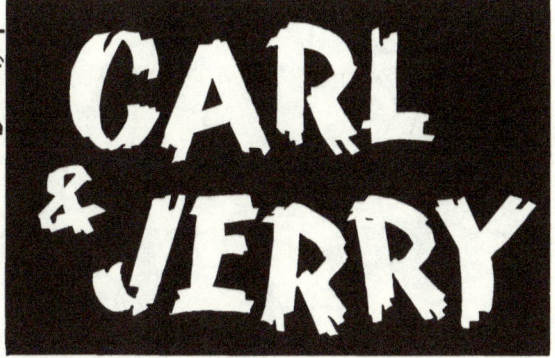

TORNADO HUNTING BY TRANSISTOR

May 1955

A few minutes ago Carl had dropped into the basement laboratory and thrown himself down on the workbench while he chatted with Jerry, stretched out on the battered old couch across the room. Suddenly Jerry became silent and heaved himself up to a sitting position.

"Say," he said, trying to sit quietly so the couch springs would stop their squeaking protest, "do you hear music?"

"Music!" Carl repeated in wide-eyed surprise. "What's the matter with you, old buddy? You flipped your lid?"

"I hear music," Jerry stubbornly insisted as he got up and padded around the room, checking the receivers, hi-fi amplifier, record player, and similar equipment strewn about the room. Every few steps he stopped to listen intently. "It seems to be louder over here by the bench," he observed. "Hey! It's coming out of you!" he exclaimed and began to "frisk" him in the professional manner of a TV whodunit detective.

"Get your cotton-picking hands off me!" Carl shouted as he planted a big foot in the middle of Jerry's chest and shoved him across the room to a sitting position on the couch. "If you must know, this is what you've been hearing," he went on as he unbuttoned his shirt pocket and pulled forth a flat little bakelite case not much larger than a pack of king-size cigarettes. He turned a small knurled knob that protruded through a slot in the case, and the whisper of music rose to a volume that filled the room.

"Hey," Jerry exclaimed with mounting enthusiasm, "I'll bet that's the transistor radio I saw in the January 1955 *Popular Electronics*."

"Right!" Carl proudly admitted. "You're feasting your blue eyes on the very first transistor radio put on the market. This is the real thing, with a built-in loop antenna, i.f. stages, and even a.v.c. There are no tubes—just four little transistors and a crystal diode to take their place."

"I know all that," Jerry interrupted, "but how does it work?"

"What station you want to hear?" Carl asked confidently.

"Try Chicago; that's a hundred and twenty miles away."

Carl moved the little dial at the top of the case, and one after another five Chicago stations were picked up with ample volume. "And just for good measure, here's Cincinnati, a couple of hundred miles away," he said as WLW rolled in strong and clear.

"I'll be jiggered," Jerry marveled. "That sure is keen reception for the middle of the day. It changes my thinking about those new transistor receivers that are coming on the market. Before hearing this one, I thought they were clever toys. You know, a sort of glorified crystal set that would pick up strong local stations and not much else."

"You ain't heard nothing yet," Carl boasted. "This set came from my uncle in New York yesterday, and he sent a hearing-aid type earphone that plugs into this little hole in the side of the case. When it's plugged in, the speaker's cut out. Last night after I went to bed I was using the earphone to do some DXing. It must have been a hot night on the broadcast band. New York, Atlanta, New Orleans, and Dallas rolled in like our local station; but I was really floored when I picked up two stations in Mexico City. I stayed with them until they announced to be sure. It made me feel kind of funny to be sitting there in the middle of the bed, holding in the palm of my hand a complete receiver on which I was hearing Spanish singing commercials from 2500 miles away whooping it up for *Coca Cola*—especially when I knew the loop antenna was no bigger than a stick of chewing gum."

"If I remember right," Jerry mused, "that set draws about four mils from a 22½-volt battery. Two thousand, five hundred miles on something with less than a tenth of a watt of power consumption is pretty good mileage. Say, we could put on a real mind-reading act with that thing. You could wear the earphone under a turban, and I could go out in the audience with a small concealed transmitter. Then you could hear and answer the questions people whispered to me. We gotta work on that."

"Okay," Carl agreed, "but that's not really what I came over to talk about. Get a load of that static. It's building up so bad on 75 meters that I had to QRT on a QSO I was having with W9YVS up in Garrett. Bert was telling me about tornado static. He says that for several years he's been able to tell whenever there's a tornado within three or four hundred miles just by listening to his receiver. He says that when a tornado is doing its stuff, it makes a peculiar kind of static. Instead of individual crashes, he describes it as being sort of a continuous noise, like the sound of loose gravel falling on a tin roof."

"And he's right!" Jerry exclaimed. "That fits in with an article I was reading in the newspaper. A professor by the name of Dr. H. L. Jones at Oklahoma A & M has been studying tornado static since 1947. Those high voltage lightning discharges he calls *sferics*, from the word 'atmospherics.' As a storm goes up in intensity, the frequency of the discharges increases; and the number of them that takes place in any second can be used as a guide as to whether or not a tornado is in the thunderstorm. Fifteen strokes a second indicates hail, and that the storm is building toward a tornado. Twenty-three strokes per second means tornado activity is going on and when twenty-six strokes are recorded, the tornado has been spawned."

"How did he count the strokes?" Carl asked.

"By displaying the lightning discharge on an oscilloscope and taking a picture with an automatic camera every time there was a lightning stroke. At the same time another camera took a picture of a radar scope that showed where the storm center was located. With this gadget going twenty-four hours a day, all Professor Jones had to do was to wait until a cyclone passed near the radar station and then look at the pictures when the tornado was in business. In Oklahoma you sometimes don't have to wait too long; and he got some dandy pictures. One funnel was obliging enough to start forming right over the station!

"He found that not only the number of strokes was important, but also their nature. A tornado turned out a large percentage of high-frequency sferics with scope pictures altogether different from the low-frequency patterns seen during an ordinary thunderstorm. These high-frequency jobs appeared *only* when there was tornado activity— Hey! You're not listening to me."

"I was just thinking," Carl said slowly. "A thunderstorm is a comparatively small-diameter affair, isn't it?"

"Yes, but what do you have in mind?"

"Did you ever notice that when a thunderstorm is coming on you can see the effect of each lightning stroke as lines across a TV screen?"

"Sure."

"Well, why couldn't we use the directional characteristics of your Yagi-type TV antenna and your antenna rotating motor to get a rough idea of the location of a storm and the direction in which it was moving?"

"Hm-m-m," Jerry said with a thoughtful frown on his round face. "I can't seem to think of any good reason. Let's try it."

In a couple of minutes the boys were upstairs and had Jerry's TV set going. The volume was turned down to quiet the noise and the receiver was set to a blank channel as Jerry swung the antenna about with the rotator.

"You get the best lines when you're aiming south," Carl observed, "but that's about all you can tell. The front receiving lobe is too wide to do any pin-pointing."

"Let's try turning the antenna broadside to the storm," Jerry suggested. "A Yagi antenna has very sharp nulls off the sides. We'll adjust it for minimum noise reception with one side pointed in the general direction of south."

"Hey, now you're in business!" Carl exclaimed. "See; there's just

two short periods of time as the antenna swings around when the lines go away down."

"Let's see now," Jerry said. "Our antenna indicator says the antenna is pointing about ten degrees north of due east; so that should mean the side of the antenna we're interested in is pointing about ten degrees to the east of south. That would put the storm center somewhere along a line from here through a point a little to the east of Indianapolis—"

"Listen!" Carl interrupted as he suddenly noticed the little transistor receiver grinding away in his shirt pocket. The crashes of static it had been giving off suddenly merged into a continuous roar that sounded very much like the interference created by an old-fashioned electric razor or a food mixer. "Golly!" he exclaimed, "that sounds exactly like the kind of static Bert was telling me about."

"Can you get any broadcast stations?" Jerry asked.

Carl moved the little dial to the frequency of the local broadcast station, and it came in clearly with only an occasional weak scratching sound heard under the powerful signal. Jerry returned to his TV rotator control and found that now the continuous lines across the face of the tube made it comparatively easy to find a very sharp null; but he also noticed he had to keep nudging the antenna to the north to maintain the null.

"That storm must be moving to the east," he remarked over his shoulder to Carl, only to find that he was no longer standing there. "What are you doing over there at the window?" he demanded as he caught sight of Carl holding the curtains aside and peering out to the south.

"Well, it's thisaway," Carl drawled; "tracking tornados is all well and good, but I just want to be sure the tracks don't get too fresh. If I see anything out there that looks the least bit like a funnel-shaped cloud,

I'm going to break the sound barrier getting back into that basement. Just don't get in my way."

"Pooh!" Jerry scoffed. "Bert has your imagination all fired up. We've just been hearing a bad thunderstorm. Even that seems to be subsiding. I notice the grinding noise is quieting down in the TV set, and all I hear are isolated crashes of static again—"

He was interrupted by the announcer breaking in on the musical program coming out of Carl's shirt pocket: "Ladies and gentlemen, we interrupt this program to bring you a special bulletin. A small tornado has just been reported by a pilot flying near Indianapolis. He reports when he first sighted the tornado that it was about eight miles due east of that city and was traveling in an east-northeasterly direction. When he was watching the funnel, it was clearing the earth by an estimated five hundred feet, and he could observe no damage in its wake. After a few minutes it disintegrated and was not seen to reform. Keep tuned to this station for further news as it develops. We now return to our program of recorded music."

"Holy cow!" Jerry breathed, "that *was* a tornado we heard."

"Well, anyway, we've learned two things," Jerry remarked as he switched off the TV set and pulled the line cord from the wall as he always did when there was danger of a thunderstorm. "First, a TV set and an antenna rotator can be used to determine the general direction and progress of a thunderstorm or tornado. Secondly, a tornado *does* put out a special kind of static that is easy to recognize once you've heard it." —30—

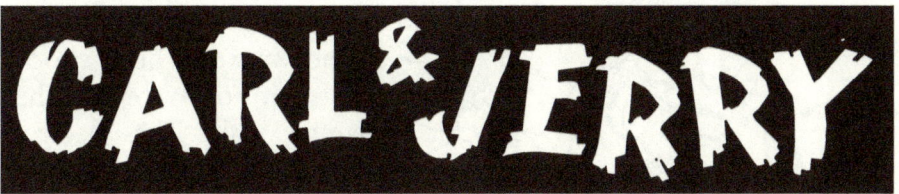

HOW TV WORKS

June 1955

It was hot, and Jerry certainly was not hurrying at his job of washing the family car. From time to time he looked wistfully across the back yard at the house of his friend, Carl Anderson; but he never presented himself—never, that is, until Jerry had given the gleaming hood a final flick of the chamois and collapsed on the ground to mop his sweating round face.

Then Carl ambled out the back door of his house and slowly strolled over to where Jerry was sprawled on the grass beside the garage. "Rather warm today, isn't it?" he remarked politely as he stifled a bored yawn.

"I wouldn't know," Jerry grunted. "I've been too busy to notice. Of course, if one is too lazy to help one's buddy out, and if all one does is sit around the house like a lounge lizard, I suppose one might think it hot."

"Now don't get your nose hard," Carl said with a disarming grin. "I made up my mind that this was one time you were not going to rope me into helping you. For once," he boasted, tapping his temple with a forefinger, "I used the old bean and stayed in the house until you were finished. Anyway, I was doing some heavy thinking. I was trying to figure out exactly how a TV picture is made to appear on the screen of a receiver."

"Nothing hard about that," Jerry scoffed, as he pulled up a handful of grass and threw it at his chum.

"Okay," Carl challenged; "suppose you fill me in on the subject."

"In the first place," Jerry began, as he picked up the garden hose and opened the nozzle, "you have what is called an *electron-gun* structure at

the very back of the picture tube neck. This gun emits a stream of electrons in the same way this hose shoots a stream of water at that garage wall. The electron beam is focused to produce the smallest possible round beam of electrons just as I adjust the nozzle here to produce a small round stream of water. "When the stream of electrons strikes the fluorescent material coated on the inside of the picture tube face—the part you call the screen—the material glows and gives off light at the point of impact. Generally speaking, the more electrons in the beam, the brighter is this spot of light on the screen.

"Keep in mind that the electron beam current in a picture tube corresponds to the plate current in an ordinary radio tube. In the picture tube the fluorescent screen takes the place of the radio tube plate. In a vacuum tube you put a fixed negative bias voltage on the grid to make the resting plate current assume a certain value, but in a picture tube you establish a similar bias voltage level with the *brightness control, so* the beam current has a certain static *no picture* value. In a vacuum tube you then apply a signal to the control grid and that causes the plate current to move up and down in accordance with the amplitude and polarity of the signal voltage. In the picture tube, the beam current follows the picture signal voltage applied to the control grid in the same manner. The only difference is that in a radio tube circuit you have to use meters to observe the changes in plate current; but in a picture tube you can observe the variations in beam current as an increase or decrease in fluorescent brightness on the screen."

"I'm still with you," Carl drawled, as he kept his eyes closed behind his horn-rimmed glasses. "But all that does is produce a bright spot. What I want to know is how a picture is made."

"You've got to learn to crawl before you walk," Jerry admonished. "That little spot of light is our paint brush, and we must be able to move the beam producing it to any portion of the screen. What's more, the movement of this beam must be done in a uniform and systematic manner. Suppose this portion of the garage wall I'm marking off with water from the hose is our picture tube screen, and the stream of water represents the electron beam inside the tube. Now I'll start over here in the upper left-hand corner of our screen and move the beam across to the right. Then I jerk it back very quickly, move the stream down a little, and draw another line below the first. Then I draw another line below that, and so on until I reach the bottom of the screen. Next I go back up and draw another series of lines *between* those already drawn until I again reach the bottom. Because the screen material will continue to glow for a small fraction of a second after the electron beam has moved on and because of the persistence of human vision, the result of this rapid back-and-forth and slower up-and-down deflection of the electron beam results in a *raster* of a number of interlaced parallel horizontal lines on the face of the picture tube."

"How many lines?" Carl wanted to know.

"The first trip down across the face of the tube the beam draws 262 ½ lines to complete the first *field* as it is called. Then the beam goes back to the top and draws 262 ½ more lines between those already drawn to make the second field. The total number of lines drawn in the two fields that are combined to make a single picture or *frame* as it is called, is 525."

"I'll count 'em sometime and see," Carl said skeptically.

"Well, don't expect to get exactly 525," Jerry warned. "That back and forth motion keeps right on going while the beam is being returned from the bottom of the picture to the top between fields, but you do not see these retrace lines because they are blanked out. About twenty-five lines per frame are lost in this manner."

"How is that beam moved back and forth and up and down?" Carl quizzed.

"That's a little complicated to explain in simple terms, but I'll try," Jerry said manfully. "You know that voltmeter I have that has a zero-center scale. When we pass a current through the meter coil in one direction, the pointer moves in one direction; but if we reverse the direction of the current, the pointer is deflected to the opposite side of the scale. Reversing the direction of the current through the meter coil reversed the polarity of the magnetic field produced by that coil; and this field reacted with the fixed magnetic field of the field magnets in the meter to cause the pointer's action.

"A coil called a *deflection yoke* is divided into two parts and these two series-connected coils are arranged opposite one another along the neck of the picture tube at a point along the path of the electron beam on its way to the screen. Now a beam of electrons creates a magnetic field about it just as a stream of electrons, representing a direct current through a wire, creates a field about that wire that can be detected with a compass. You remember we did that experiment in physics class when we were studying the right-hand rule. If we put a current through our series-connected coils, they set up a magnetic field in the portion of the tube neck between them. The magnetic field of the electron beam and the magnetic field produced by these deflection yoke coils react with one another in such a way that the electron beam moves in a direction which will minimize this reaction. The direction and extent of the movement of this weightless, inertia-free electron pointer depends upon the strength and direction of the current through the deflection yoke coils.

"By making the current through the deflection yoke take the form of a saw-tooth—a current pulse that builds up gradually from zero to a certain value and then falls very quickly to zero again—we can make the beam move comparatively slowly from left to right across the tube face and then snap back quickly to the left side of the screen.

"A similar saw-tooth of current at a much lower frequency which is passed through another pair of deflection yoke coils mounted at right angles to the ones producing horizontal deflection makes the beam move comparatively slowly from the top of the tube to the bottom and then snap back to the top again. These two magnetic fields, exerting their combined influence on the electron beam simultaneously, cause it to describe the line-drawing process, or *scanning*, as it is called, that we were talking about."

"How many of these frames or pictures occur in a minute?"

"It's easier to measure them by the second. Sixty fields, or thirty complete frames, occur every second. Breaking each picture up into two fields cuts down the possibility of flicker and also has some other advantages. Movie cameras in theatres use the same basic system to reduce flicker. The film speed in those machines is twenty-four frames per second, but each frame is projected twice to produce a total of forty-eight picture-showings per second."

"That little old spot of light on the picture tube must be hustling."

"You're not kidding. I figured out one time that on a twenty-one inch tube the spot of light must be traveling at a line-drawing speed of about 16,000 miles per hour. The speed during retrace action is about ten times that."

"Okay, let's get on with it," Carl prodded. "All you've produced so far is a raster of 500 parallel lines of brightness on our screen."

"*Muy bien,* Buddy, but you can help from here on in," Jerry said. "You can be the modulator for our TV transmitter. Throw a kink in that hose and when I say 'cut,' stop the water until I say 'open.' This fresh section of garage wall I'm marking off with the hose will be our screen. The picture we receive will be the simple one of a black telephone pole standing out in a snow storm. Remember the wet wall indicates white on our screen and the dry portion represents black.

"At the transmitter," Jerry went on, "there is a tube in the camera that is a sort of miniature version of the picture tube in the receiver. The image of the scene being photographed is focused on the screen of this tube, and this image is scanned by an electron beam just as we described. What's more, the scanning beam in the camera tube and the one in the receiver picture tube are kept locked exactly in step with even more precision than the movements of the June Taylor Dancers on the Jackie Gleason show."

"Now I'm beginning to get a picture," Carl murmured with his eyes still closed.

"When the scanning beam of the camera tube strikes a light portion of the picture, it causes the amplitude of the transmitter carrier to be reduced; when it moves to a dark picture element, the carrier amplitude increases. How much the carrier decreases or increases depends upon how light or dark that particular picture element is.

"In our TV receiver this increase or decrease of carrier strength is translated into increasing or decreasing negative signal voltage applied to the control grid of the picture tube. Keep in mind that a change in this voltage is immediately apparent as a change in brightness in the line or lines being traced on the screen at the instant the change takes place. Holding all this in mind, let's start scanning our garage-

wall picture. First I start at the upper left-hand corner with the stream of water. As I get to about the middle of our screen, I say, 'cut!'"

Obediently Carl kinked the hose sharply and the water stopped. Jerry moved the nozzle over a bit and commanded, "Open," and Carl released the pressure so that the drawing of the line could be completed. In this manner several interrupted wet lines were drawn across the garage wall inside the rough rectangle Jerry had marked off with the stream. Then the water was cut off while Jerry went back to the top of his "screen" and started drawing another set of interrupted lines between those already drawn. The result was. a completely wet rectangle with a rather crude vertical dry stripe up the center. Between directions to Carl, Jerry continued to lecture.

"The directions I'm giving you are the ones given to the transmitter by the pickup tube in the television camera. These directions are passed on to the TV receiver through its antenna, and inside the receiver are passed right to the electron beam inside the picture tube. That means that when the scanning beam of the camera tube is moving across a light portion of the scene, the TV picture tube is showing a bright line. When the camera tube scan ning beam is on a coal-black picture element, the beam of the picture tube is cut off and the screen is allowed to go black. In short, since these two beams are in exact synchronization, whatever is *seen* by the camera tube scanning beam is *shown* on the face of the picture tube by variations in the intensity of its beam. Gray shades are portrayed simply by reducing the intensity of the picture tube beam without actually cutting it off entirely. The nearer the voltage applied to the control grid of the picture tube approaches the cutoff voltage, the dimmer is the line drawn by the beam and the darker is the shade of gray. Well, here goes the last line of our picture. What do you think—?"

He never got to finish his question. At this instant the kinked hose in Carl's hands suddenly gave way and threw a great spray of water over both boys and over the gleaming automobile against which they had been leaning.

"Hey, the modulator's busted!" Carl yelled as he scrambled for the valve to shut off the hose. It was too late. The freshly washed car was splattered all over from the shower it had received.

Jerry surveyed the damage ruefully for a moment and then picked up two pieces of chamois skin and held one out to Carl.

"Be my guest!" he invited.

—30—

ULTRASONIC ROMANCE

July 1955

The shadowy coolness of Jerry's basement lab was a welcome relief from the shimmering heat outside. As Carl came in, he saw Jerry's rotund figure perched on top of a stool at the workbench, on which rested a delicate horn pan balance with a one-milligram weight in one of its pans. With a pair of tweezers, Jerry was carefully transferring some minute objects from a fruit jar lid to the other pan.

"Looks like you're really up to big business today," Carl observed. "What're you weighing, peach fuzz?"

"Nope, . . . mosquito cadavers," Jerry said, as his round face wreathed itself into an enigmatic smile.

Carl moved to the bench and peered down through his horn-rimmed glasses at the jar lid. Sure enough, in it were several rather badly mauled mosquito carcasses.

"Why?" Carl demanded.

"We-1-1-1," Jerry said hesitatingly, "It's a rather long story—"

"Never mind the buildup," Carl interrupted. "You know you're dying to tell me; so give."

"It all started a couple of nights ago. Looking out my bedroom window, I saw Norma, the girl next door, sitting on her porch-swing, blubbering and crying away. Thinking that maybe she had locked herself out of the house or something, I went down to see what was wrong.

"It developed that a character by the name of Melvin Akers, who works at the bank, has her 'snowed.' For the life of me, I can't see why, for this Melvin guy is the sort even nature hates. He's allergic to anything

that grows. He breaks out in a rash if anyone even mentions onions or radishes. She swears he can get ivy poisoning just from seeing the word 'ivy' in print.

"Even so, she has her mind dead set on marrying the creep; and that night she thought she practically had the job done. Melvin was in a rare mood—for him—with nothing to take his attention off her; and he had even made a couple of cracks about how pretty her hair looked in the moonlight.

"They sat down in the porch swing, and she started rehearsing mentally just how she was going to say 'I will' to his proposal. Then, all of a sudden, Melvin began slapping at his face and ankles, and suddenly stood up and said he had to leave. He's one of those people mosquitoes love to bite, and the bites swell up on him. So, he had to get home quickly and use some special ointment on them.

"That was why she was crying. She said she'd pinned her hopes on this moonlit porch swing setting all spring; and now that it had failed, she just knew Melvin would never propose."

"Why doesn't she try citronella?" Carl asked.

"I thought of that, too, but she says the odor clashes with her *Sweet Surrender* perfume, in which she has invested no small sum and which she is sure plays a big part in giving old Melvin the business. I told her I'd try to see if I couldn't think of something to help her."

"How come you're so eager to play Cupid?" Carl asked suspiciously; "although I must admit you've got the figure for it. You going soft on this gal, too?"

"You got rocks in your head?" Jerry demanded witheringly. "She's practically an old woman. I'll bet she's 22 or 23 if she's a day. It's just that I don't like having someone bawling under my window when I'm trying to sleep. And then, her problem appeals to my scientific curiosity."

"How about Melvin? Don't you think it's playing it kind of low down to help trap a fellow man?"

"That bothered me a little until I happened to remember he was the local joker who wrote to the FCC and said he was sure we radio amateurs were interfering with his TV reception. All his trouble was being caused by an old-fashioned carbon filament light bulb in his basement. Some of those old bulbs act like miniature TV transmitters and cause interference to crawl up and down the picture."

"He deserves to get married!" was Carl's prompt, harsh judgment; "but how are you going to help with the mosquito situation?"

"I got an idea from something I read in *Radio & TV News* two or three years ago. You know sound waves can exert severe stress on objects that are resonant to the frequency of the sound. Remember how some opera singers can shatter a wine glass just by holding the right high note? Well, I think I can produce an ultrasonic sound wave at a frequency that will vibrate a mosquito violently and destroy him without people being able to hear the sound.

"Yesterday I borrowed a high-power movie sound system tweeter speaker from a projectionist friend of mind and hooked it across the output of my hi-fi amplifier. This amplifier has frequency response clear up to 100,000 cycles; so when I ran my audio signal generator into the front end of the amplifier, I got considerable power output from the speaker above the range of hearing. To check this, I suspended a tiny pith ball on a light thread in the path of the narrow cone of sound put out by the speaker and then varied the frequency of the signal generator. At certain ultrasonic frequencies, the ball was jerked back and forth so violently by the inaudible sound waves that it looked blurred. I'm sure that if I can hit just the right frequency I can exert several G's of stress on a mosquito and shake him loose from his wings!"

"Why are you weighing the mosquitoes?"

"To get the average weight to use in the acceleration graphs and formulas for vibratory motion that I found down at the library. They're pretty hard to use, but if I do it right I should be able to figure out just the right frequency to apply maximum stress to a single mosquito."

As he talked, Jerry finally got the scales to show a satisfactory balance; and then he carefully counted the dead mosquitoes in the pan. Next he reached for his battered slide rule, made a few calculations, and jotted down some figures on a pad.

"We-1-1," he finally said hesitatingly, "if I've not slipped somewhere, it looks as though a frequency of about 19,000 cycles ought to do it. Tonight I'll run that frequency into the amplifier and direct the cone of sound from the tweeter speaker right at Norma's porch swing from my upstairs window. She says she'll maneuver Melvin into position there promptly at 10:30 if she has to chloroform him. I'll keep the mosquitoes at bay with my supersonic ray until Norma and her *Sweet Surrender* perfume have done their dirty work."

"You playing an electronic Cupid is something I've got to see," Carl announced. "Reserve me a seat up in your room tonight. I'll be over right after that 9:30 shoot-em-up TV program."

He was as good as his word, and the two boys squatted on the floor by the window of the hot, darkened bedroom for almost an hour before they heard the picket gate of the house next door click open and shut, and caught sight of two figures walking onto the vine-hung front porch. Jerry already had the amplifier warmed up; and as he heard the rhythmic squeaking of the porch swing chains, he flipped on the oscillator that had been preset to the ultrasonic frequency. The shift in the fluorescent blue glow on the glass envelopes of the amplifier output tubes indicated that they were delivering power. No sound was heard from the speaker, however, and there was no halt in the rhythmic squeaking of the swing chains.

"Well, at least Melvin can't hear the sound," Jerry whispered hoarsely as he stared down at the darkened porch. Just as he said this, there was an anguished howl from below, and a frantic ball of white erupted from beneath the porch and ran crazily about the moonlit yard.

"Holy cow!" Carl gasped, "it's Bosco! What's the matter with him?"

Before Jerry could answer, Melvin's trembling voice floated up to them: "It's a mad dog!" he shrieked. Then he burst from the shadow of the porch, and with two giant steps reached the picket fence and vaulted nimbly over it. He alighted on the sidewalk running, and as

his staccato footsteps died away in the distance, Jerry reached over and switched off the oscillator. Instantly Bosco's howling stopped.

"Bosco certainly fouled that up," Jerry said sadly. "Dogs can hear sounds too high-pitched for human beings, and that high frequency note must have been pretty painful to poor Bosco's ears.

The two boys went downstairs and across the yard. To their astonishment, they heard the sound of almost hysterical laughter coming from the porch, and then Norma ran down the steps, threw her arms about them, and kissed each squirming boy soundly on the cheek.

"I'll never, never forget how funny Melvin looked as he went over that fence," she finally managed to gasp. "And I want you boys to know I'll never forget what you've done for me. I guess I felt sorry for Melvin because he seemed to have so much trouble, and I foolishly thought I was in love with him; but I certainly couldn't love anyone who would run off and leave me alone with a mad dog ... I don't know how you did it, but you're wonderful!"

As she said this, she stooped down and picked up Bosco, still pawing gingerly at his ears, and gave the dog a big hug; then she went into the house, giggling happily.

"Women!" Carl said disgustedly, as he rubbed the lipstick print off his cheek vigorously with the back of his hand.

"Check," Jerry agreed. "I suppose we may as well go to bed now, but I'm coming over the first thing in the morning to see if there are any wingless mosquito fuselages lying around under that swing."

Carl took a couple of steps and then turned around. "Hey, Jer," he said thoughtfully, "I wonder if you'd promise me something."

"Sure thing. What is it?"

"Well, if I should ever become so weak-minded as to think I want a girlfriend, just let me manage my love life all by myself, will you? Please don't try to help me!"   —30—

ALL ABOUT TV ANTENNAS

August 1955

The hot August sun beat down on the two boys climbing up the steep path. Lanky, athletic Carl Anderson scarcely breathed hard as he forged steadily up the hill; but behind him his overly plump chum, Jerry Bishop, puffed like a steam locomotive as he toiled along the steep ascent. In spite of his noisy effort, Jerry kept falling farther and farther behind, and finally he came to a full stop and collapsed in the shade of a huge boulder beside the path.

"How come you're dropping anchor there, Blimp Boy?" Carl called down. "We've still got a quarter of a mile to go to the top."

"I can never make it," Jerry gasped feebly. "Go on without me. Just say my spirit was willing but the flesh was weak. Leave me a dozen sandwiches or so to make my last moments comfortable."

"Not a chance!" Carl interrupted harshly. "I coaxed you on this hike to sweat some of the fat off you, and off it comes—one way or another. We agreed to eat, you will remember, when we got to the top of the hill. Well, if I've got to go on by myself, I'm going to take the lunch with me and eat it—all of it —up there just as we planned."

"You wouldn't *dare!*" Jerry cried, with the quick instinctive anger of a hungry dog who sees his bone suddenly snatched from him.

"Oh no?" Carl said tauntingly, as he squatted on his heels and opened the lunch basket he was carrying. Very deliberately, he removed a thick paper-wrapped sandwich and slowly pulled out the toothpick thrust through it.

With a snarl of mixed hunger and rage, Jerry leaped to his feet and charged up the path toward his tormenter. Carl barely had time to toss

the sandwich back into the hamper and scramble upward out of Jerry's clawing reach. The latter was so incensed by the horrifying prospect of Carl's eating all the lunch that he did not slacken his pace and the two boys arrived at the top almost neck and neck.

"You made it!" Carl congratulated, as he flung himself at full length on the thick grass beneath a tree.

For a minute, Jerry stood over him with his face still wearing its menacing scowl, but then as he looked about and realized he had actually reached the summit, his round countenance broke into a pleased grin and he sat down abruptly beside his friend.

"We better cool off a little before we eat," Carl suggested. "It certainly is a wonderful view, isn't it?"

"It sure is," Jerry agreed, with his head buried in the picnic hamper. "Now that we've cooled off for at least a couple of hundred seconds, let's eat. Do you want your tenderloin sandwich with or without mustard?"

There was little conversation for the next few minutes as the boys waded through the assorted sandwiches, hard-boiled eggs, and fresh fruit that Carl's mother had provided. Finally, though, when they were munching their chocolate bar dessert, Carl said lazily:

"Jer, look at all those TV antennas down there. Hardly two of them are alike; yet they're all intended to receive the same stations. How come there are so many different kinds?"

Jerry pillowed his head on his clasped hands and stared up at the fleecy white clouds drifting across the blue sky overhead. "To answer that properly really takes a lot of doing," he said slowly. "You almost have to go into the subject of how TV antennas work."

"So let's go into it," Carl promptly urged. "I've got the time, and you think you've got the information."

"When TV broadcasting first started," Jerry began, "the receivers were invariably close to the transmitter, and the engineers simply adapted the old standby short-wave receiving antenna, the half-wave dipole. This is simply a conductor which is an electrical half-wavelength long at the frequency being received, and which is cut in two at the middle so that each half feeds into one part of a two-conductor feedline, such as a twisted pair, coaxial cable, or piece of twin-lead. In radio work, the conductor is usually wire; but since a half wave is only a matter of a few feet on the TV frequencies, the TV antenna was made up of a couple of pieces of aluminum tubing secured to a center block of insulation."

"I don't see anything like that down there," Carl remarked as he raised himself on an elbow and looked down at the rooftop antennas.

"No, that simple antenna didn't last long because it had several serious flaws. For one thing, it had a front-to-back ratio of 1 to 1. By that I mean its horizontal reception pattern looked like a figure '8.' While practically no reception was had off either end of the dipole, identical reception lobes extended out from either side. If you called one side the 'front' of the antenna and pointed it at a station, another station at the rear would be equally favored in reception. As more and more stations came on the air, forcing many to share the same channel in nearby cities, this became a serious defect. Secondly, the output impedance of the dipole is about 72 ohms, an inconvenient value for matching to low-cost, low-loss transmission lines."

"I don't dig this impedance-matching business as well as I might," Carl admitted.

"I figured. Every piece of equipment that generates, carries, or receives r.f. currents has a certain amount of built-in opposition to the flow of those currents that is called 'impedance,'" Jerry explained, beginning to enjoy his role of lecturer. "In order to transfer the maximum amount of power or signal from one piece of equipment to another, their respective impedances must be equal or 'matched.' If the TV antenna is not matched to the feedline and if the feedline is not matched to the receiver, you not only lose a lot of signal but the mismatch is likely to generate annoying ghosts in the picture. Most TV sets are built with an antenna input impedance of 300 ohms. Low cost and efficient twin-lead designed to match this also has a 'surge' impedance, as it is called, of 300 ohms. But if you have to feed a 72-ohm half-wave dipole antenna into the end of this 300-ohm feedline, you have a 4 to 1 mismatch."

"And I guess a 52-ohm coax line would be worse?"

"It can be done, and some receivers have a 52-ohm input for this line, but it is much more expensive than twin-lead and has a much higher loss than a good grade of dry twin-lead. It was easier to change the dipole so that its impedance would match the inexpensive 300-ohm flat line."

"How did they cut that caper?"

"Just by placing another conductor a half wavelength long three or four inches above the dipole and connecting its ends to the outside ends of the dipole. This changed the simple dipole into a 'folded dipole,' with several important advantages. For one thing, the antenna impedance was quadrupled so that it was almost an exact match for the 300-ohm line. Secondly, the frequency response of the folded dipole is much wider than that of the simple dipole."

"Wait up!" Carl commanded. "What's this jive about widening the frequency response?"

"The dipole delivered maximum received signal strength only on the channel for which it was cut. Signals on adjacent channels excited much less response in the antenna, and signals from channels still farther removed from the antenna's resonant frequency produced still less response. Since the antenna responded only to signals close to its resonant frequency, we say it had a *narrow* bandwidth. The folded dipole responds much more strongly to signals on adjacent channels, so we say it has a *wider* bandwidth. Catch?"

"Roger. With a wide-band antenna, you can receive several channels on the same antenna. With a narrow-band job, you can receive only one channel well."

"I do believe you're getting brighter!" Jerry said sarcastically. "At any rate, the folded dipole still did not have all the answers. Especially, it did not prevent receiving a station just as well off the back of the antenna as the front. To correct this fault, TV design engineers borrowed the Yagi antenna radio hams had been using on 10 and 20 meters for years. To change a folded dipole into a Yagi, you mount the

dipole horizontally on a long horizontal boom. On this boom, parallel to the dipole, you mount several other metal rods or tubes called 'parasitic elements' because they have no direct connection to the 'driven element' connected to the feedline. Parasitic elements on the front part of the boom are called 'directors,' and they are a trifle shorter than the driven element and must be mounted at certain critical distances ahead of that element. At the rear of the boom, also at a critical distance, is mounted a parasitic element called a 'reflector' that is somewhat longer than the driven element.

"A complete Yagi may have all the way from 3 to 12 or more elements. Directors concentrate the received signal on the driven element in much the same way that lenses focus light. The reflector reinforces this action in the same manner that a polished surface will reflect and concentrate light rays on a particular spot. The end result is that the reception of a signal arriving from the front of the antenna is greatly improved and response to a signal arriving from any point of the compass *except* the front is cut way down."

"Sounds like the perfect answer to the TV antenna problem."

"For single-channel reception, it's hard to beat—but there's the rub. In its conventional form, a Yagi is a very narrow-band affair, good only for reception of the single channel for which it was designed. Lately, however, the engineers have given the old Yagi a new look by working it over into what is known as the broadband Yagi—capable of yielding good signal strength and excellent front-to-back ratio on all 12 v.h.f. TV channels. This is done by using more than one driven element and by carefully adjusting the length and spacing of the parasitic elements so that they do double or triple duty, effectively producing the equivalent of several different Yagi antennas mounted on a single boom. That antenna over there, next to the church, is called an 'Interceptor,' and is a good example of this design."

"How about those jobs with the elements sticking out every which way? I think they're called *conicals*."

"Well, going back to our original dipole, increasing the physical size of the dipole elements will widen the frequency response. Theoretically, the best way to do this is to use metal cones mounted tip-to-tip for the elements. The cones can be flattened into triangular sheets of metal without much loss of effectiveness, and this is actually done on the u.h.f. channels. The resulting dipoles are called 'bow-ties' because of their appearance, and are usually mounted in front of a reflecting metal grid or inside the jaws of two such grids edge-connected at a 90° angle to form what is known as a 'corner reflector.'

"On the v.h.f. channels, where wavelengths are measured in feet instead of inches, a bow-tie of proper dimensions would be too bulky and expensive and have too much wind resistance. However, metal rods or tubes that preserve the outline of the bow-tie, and that might be considered the skeleton of the original cones, serve almost as well. By inclining the skeleton wings of this 'conical' dipole slightly forward to form a shallow funnel, reception on the higher channels is improved. TV signals are directed in toward the feedline point in much the same way that sound waves are collected by an old-fashioned hearing trumpet. A skeleton bow-tie reflector is usually mounted behind the conical antenna to improve the front-to-back ratio. To get still more strength in fringe areas, it is a common practice to stack two, four, or even more of these conical 'bays,' as they are called, one above the other on the same mast, and connect them to a common feedline. To insure that the signals picked up by the several bays actually reinforce instead of buck each other, it's necessary that bays be mounted the proper distance apart and that they be connected together with special 'stacking harnesses.'"

"Any more TV antennas?" Carl asked drowsily.

"Lots more, but you'd never stay awake to hear about them," Jerry observed tartly. "Some antenna manufacturers depend upon stacking several dipole-and-reflector bays vertically for increased gain. Half-wave elements, properly phased, may be mounted side by side and several such bays stacked to form what is called a 'collinear array.' The appearance of such an antenna, together with a reflecting screen, has given rise to its popular nickname of 'the bedspring antenna.' Other manufacturers combine Yagi and conical antennas on a single boom, hoping to get the benefits of both from this marriage."

"What's meant by antenna gain?"

"That's the ratio between the signal voltage delivered by the antenna to the feedline on a certain channel and the voltage delivered by a reference dipole antenna cut to the frequency of that channel and mounted in the same spot. This ratio is expressed in decibels. For example, if the antenna under test delivers twice as much signal voltage as does the reference dipole on Channel 6, we say it has a 6-db gain on that channel. If it delivers four times the voltage, it has a 12-db gain."

"What characteristics would you say the perfect TV antenna should have?"

"First, it should have high gain; second, it should maintain this gain across all v.h.f. and u.h.f. channels with no peaks or dips; third, it should present a consistent 300-ohm impedance to the feedline on all frequencies; fourth, it should have a single, narrow reception lobe and should present infinite rejection to signals arriving from the side or rear; and finally, it should be cheap, light, and easily mounted, with a low wind resistance and a beautiful appearance."

"Sounds like quite an order."

"It is, especially when you realize that antenna gain, bandwidth, front-to-back ratio, and impedance are all closely interlocked so that you cannot vary one of them without changing all the others. And right there you have your answer as to why there are so many different kinds of antennas. Each manufacturer tries a different compromise in his approach to this ideal antenna. One may stress high maximum gain or front-to back ratio; another advertises price and appearance; still another may boast that the response curve of his antenna has no sharp dips and valleys in it—something especially important in an antenna used for color TV reception. Each advertising claim appeals to a certain group of customers who feel that the stressed characteristic is just what they need to solve their reception troubles. If it doesn't, then they are ready to try another new antenna, always hoping they will eventually come across the perfect TV antenna which will insure perfect reception all the time."

"You sound a little cynical about this."

"Not really. I know how important it is to have a good antenna, especially in a weak-signal area; but I also know for a fact that the TV antenna can only do so much. It cannot receive a signal that just isn't there; nor can it compensate, beyond a certain point, for a poor receiver. The TV antenna is like the automatic choke on a car; it gets a lot of blame for 'sins' for which it isn't guilty."

Carl rose and brushed the grass from the seat of his pants.

"Well, I guess we had better be starting for home, Marconi. Do you think you will be able to totter down the hill or had I better just roll you like a barrel?"

"Don't get smart with me," Jerry said, as he struggled to his feet, trying not to wince at the protest from his sore muscles. "Just don't get in my way going down like you did coming up."   —30—

ELECTRIC SHOCK

September 1955

August had been a pretty hot month and now September was starting out the same way. Even down in Jerry Bishop's basement laboratory it was warm, and the youth puttering at his workbench was barefooted and wearing only a shirt and shorts. His pal, Carl Anderson, was seated on the bench swinging his long legs idly back and forth as he watched his chubby friend working on a radio receiver.

"The shielded loop antenna fastened to the back of this set is really directional," Jerry remarked, as he picked up the chassis and stepped away from the bench so that he could turn the playing receiver about. "Wups!" he said, as the tangle-shortened line cord pulled from the wall socket. He set the receiver down on the bench, untangled the cord, replaced the plug in the wall socket, picked up the set, and once more stepped away from the bench.

Suddenly his body gave a convulsive jerk and then became rigid. A low moan forced its way between his clenched teeth. The cords in his neck and in his quivering wrists stood out tautly beneath the skin. His staring eyes looked agonizingly at his friend and then shifted imploringly over to the receiver a.c. plug in the wall socket.

Carl, whose widening eyes had been staring through his horn-rimmed glasses at the strange behavior of his companion, finally realized what was wrong; and in a single motion he leaped from the bench and tore the receiver line cord from the wall socket. In that same instant, Jerry dropped the chassis to the concrete floor with a resounding crash, tottered backward and collapsed on the leather-covered couch along the wall.

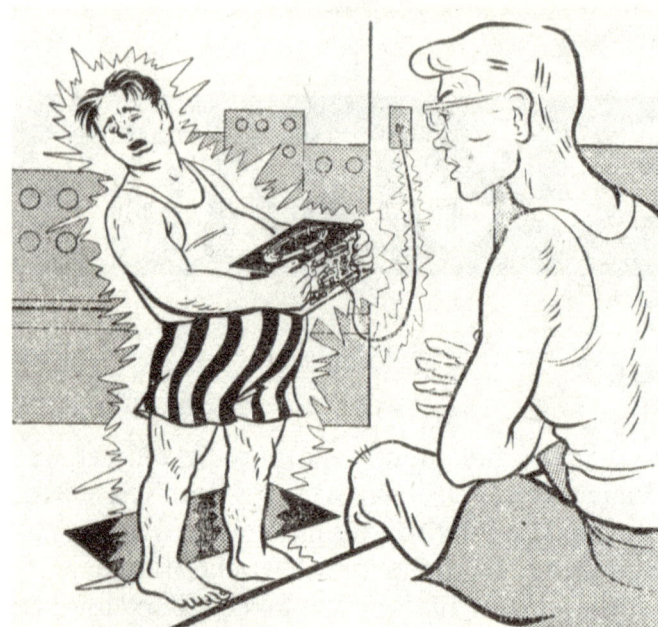

"Hey, Jer, are you all right?" Carl asked anxiously, as he bent over his friend. "What was wrong? Were you getting a shock from that set? Want me to get your folks or call a doctor? Hey, why don't you answer me?"

"Gimme a chance!" Jerry gasped, as he panted for breath through a wide-open mouth. "I'll be all right, I think, but that was mighty close."

For a few minutes he continued to gasp for breath, but gradually he began to breathe more easily and color started to return to his dead-white face. Carl, who had been watching him narrowly all the while, relaxed a little and returned to the chaffing way of talking that normally prevailed between the two fast friends.

"Heck!" he drawled, "I was hoping I might get a chance to use that new method of artificial respiration I've been practicing down at CD headquarters. Maybe," he said hopefully, "I ought to give you a little of it anyway. It won't hurt. I just sort of play you gently like an accordion."

"Keep your greasy paws off me!" Jerry warned, as he struggled to a sitting position and ruefully examined the seared white welts burned across the inside of his fingers where they had been in contact with the edges of the charged chassis. "Man, do those fingers feel hot! They must have a real fever in them. There's a nasty odor of burned flesh about 'em, too," he remarked, wrinkling his nose in distaste.

"Just wait a couple of hours until they begin to get sore," Carl encouraged.

"Well," Jerry said as he stood up rather shakily, "let's see if we can find out where I goofed. This whole thing was a shocking surprise to me, if you will allow a poor sick man a pun. I thought I was taking every precaution."

Carl set the receiver back on the bench, and the boys looked it over. Fortunately, it had landed on a corner that had doubled under and absorbed most of the shock. When a couple of tubes that had been jarred from their sockets were replaced, and the set was gingerly plugged in, it played normally.

"Pull the plug and let's see if we can reconstruct the accident," Jerry suggested. "Until we find out what went wrong, I'll be afraid to touch another electrical device of any kind. In some way the 117-volt line current must be reaching the chassis; although, in a transformer set like this, it shouldn't. Some a.c.-d.c. receivers have one side of the line connected directly to the chassis; but this is never done with transformer sets. Hm-m-m," he broke off as he reached for the ohmmeter probes, "I'll bet that's it."

"What's it?" Carl demanded. "Stop trying to sound like a pill-pusher with those knowing 'hm-m-m's' of yours."

"Each side of the line is bypassed to the chassis through a .05 mfd. capacitor," Jerry explained. "I'm thinking that one of them may be short-circuited."

Sure enough, as the probes were touched to the leads of one of the capacitors, the meter pointer indicated zero resistance. "That explains everything," Jerry said contentedly, as he tossed the probes back on the bench.

"To you, maybe; but not to me," Carl denied. "Only *one* side of the line was shorted to the chassis that both of your hands were holding. I thought you had to have a complete circuit path before electrical current would flow. Just touching one wire doesn't complete a circuit. You can't fool me. I've seen a bird roosting on a high-tension wire carrying thousands of volts."

"You're forgetting something. One side of the line coming into the house is grounded right out at the transformer. This is true of all two-wire services. For that matter, one wire of a three-wire service is grounded, too. The current was going from the ungrounded or

'hot' wire through the shorted capacitor to the chassis, then through my body and bare feet in contact with the damp cement floor, and finally back through the earth to the pole transformer out in the alley."

"You mean all you need to get a strong current flow is one wire and a good ground?"

"Sure; I'll show you." As he said this, Jerry picked up a short extension cord with a light bulb in its socket and removed the plug from the end of the twisted leads. Separating these leads, he connected a battery clamp to the end of each one. Then one clamp was clipped to the brass valve handle of a water faucet at one side of the basement, and the other was fastened to the end of a test lead. Jerry thrust the probe end of the test lead into one of the openings in the wall receptacle. Nothing happened. "That's the grounded side," Jerry remarked as he removed the test prod and thrust it into the other side of the receptacle. Instantly, the lamp in the socket glowed with normal brilliance.

"Convinced?" Jerry asked.

"Of that part," Carl admitted cautiously, "but there're still some things I don't understand. Why didn't you get a shock as soon as you touched the chassis?"

"I was standing on this long strip of rubber carpet I put in front of the bench just to avoid having contact with the earth while handling electrical equipment; but you'll recall that I stepped backward off the rubber mat just before the jolt hit me."

"But you were off the mat the first time before the plug pulled out. Why didn't you get a shock then?"

"Because the plug happened to be in the socket in such a manner that the side of the line shorted to the chassis through the capacitor was the grounded side. When I straightened out the cord and replaced the plug, I must have reversed the position of the plug prongs so that the hot side of the line was the one shorted to the chassis. Then all that protected me from shock was the rubber mat, and when I stepped off that—"

"You began to shake, rattle, and roll," Carl finished.

"You can say that again. I felt just as though my whole body was clamped in a huge vise that was squeezing tighter and tighter. You'll never know how desperately I was trying to yell at you to jerk that cord, but I couldn't get out a mumbling word."

"Have you figured out what you did wrong?"

"There's quite a list. First, standing barefooted on a damp cement floor while handling electrical equipment of any kind is just asking for trouble. Second, I should have realized that only the capacitor stood between me and a possible fatal shock; and I've replaced enough shorted capacitors to know how easily they can fail. My basic error was in not using my imagination to picture what *could* happen and then taking precautions to see that it didn't."

"Such as wearing shoes, Nature Boy?"

"Ordinary shoes would not insure safety. What I should have done, and will do immediately, is buy an isolation transformer that we'll use consistently. This is basically a simple two-winding transformer. The primary winding goes to the line, and the secondary winding feeds the device being tested. Since the secondary has no connection to the ground, there is no danger of being shocked through contact with the ground. The only way you can get shocked while using such a transformer is to contact both secondary leads simultaneously. In addition to providing this safety, the ordinary isolation transformer has tapped windings so that secondary voltages slightly above, equal to, and slightly below the line voltage can be had from the isolated secondary."

"I didn't realize you could get such a jolt from 117 volts. I always knew such a voltage would make you jump, but I didn't think it was really dangerous."

"Don't you believe it! I'll bet more people are electrocuted with the 117-volt line current than with any other potential, simply because it's so easy to contact and because it is treated with so little respect. A scientist once told me that if the skin resistance were reduced to zero a person could be killed by only six volts. Ordinarily, the oily skin provides ample protection against such low potentials, but when the skin is wet with salty perspiration as mine was, the skin resistance drops sharply; and once the current starts to burn, it quickly drops the skin resistance still more."

"Then you think those smart alecks who stick their fingers into light sockets to show how much juice they can take are not being very bright."

"That's putting it mildly! Only a jerk or a real square would do a stupid thing like that. Electricity makes a wonderful friend and servant, but it can become a vicious, lightning-fast killer if you treat it carelessly. A smart technician takes every possible precaution against getting even mild shocks, for under the right circumstances they can be fatal."

"How's that?"

"Doctors say that occasionally a comparatively mild shock can trigger the heart into quivering in a manner that interferes with its normal functioning. They believe this accounts for the deaths that sometimes occur from low-current shocks."

"Maybe that's why it's a good idea always to use only one hand when working on equipment where there's a possibility of shock."

"Check. Keeping one hand in your pocket under such circumstances is a strictly professional procedure. It avoids the possibility that a dangerous current can enter one hand and go out the other, and pass through the vulnerable chest cavity on the way across."

For a little while, there was a silence, while both boys thought about the near tragedy that had just taken place; then Jerry spoke up:

"Carl, I want you to show me how to do that new artificial respiration business you were talking about. In case of shock, artificial respiration immediately applied is the best possible first-aid treatment to use until a doctor can be reached. Getting started with the treatment just as soon as the body is freed from the current is the important factor.

A delay of only a few seconds in beginning artificial respiration may spell the difference between life and death."

"Fine!" Carl agreed; "and that gives me an idea. Let's hold regular surprise drills right here in the basement. After I've shown you how the artificial respiration is done, every few days one of us will fake being shocked. All he will have to do is touch a piece of electrical equipment that is plugged in and become rigid, just as you did. Then the other fellow will free the 'actor' from the 'hot' object, taking care not to be shocked himself. This will be done either by pulling the plug as I did, or by opening that master switch that cuts off the whole bench and all its outlets. Then, the guy doing the acting will collapse on the floor, making himself as limp as possible. The other fellow will straighten him out and start artificial respiration just as quickly as he can, and keep it up for at least a couple of minutes. If we keep doing this, we'll soon be prepared to handle a real case of shock almost automatically. Constant drilling is the best insurance against getting rattled in an emergency."

"Truer words were never spoken!" Jerry applauded. "If we use our heads and take the precautions we should, the chances are that neither of us will ever have to use first aid here in the basement; but it will be mighty comforting to know both of us can, and you never know when we may have a chance to save a life somewhere else. Working with electricity and not knowing how to apply artificial respiration is about as foolish as it would be for an explorer to start into the South American jungle without a snakebite kit."   —30—

THE GREAT BANK ROBBERY

October 1955

"Just once," Carl complained bitterly as he trudged along the road toward the approaching hills, "I'd like to take a hike without having to be a packhorse for a whole mess of electronic equipment."

"Oh, quit your griping," Jerry said good-humoredly, as he skipped lightly along carrying a bulky but obviously not very heavy box. "You're just steamed because you outsmarted yourself and elected to carry the *little* box without knowing it contained the nice heavy batteries. You're just as eager as I am to try out this portable 420 megacycle rig, and we'll never have a better opportunity than to work back to town from the top of Old Saddle Back Mountain."

"Where does this joker who is supposed to work with us live?"

"He's a new ham in town. His name is Gene Mays, and he lives in an apartment on the third floor of that building the police station is in. Gene is a real v.h.f. and u.h.f. bug and has been concentrating on the ham bands above 30 megaccyles for several years. This combination transmitter and receiver is a home-brew job of his own manufacture."

"How come you're suddenly so hopped up on u.h.f? You can't talk any farther on those frequencies than you can on 75, 40, 20, or 10 meters, can you?"

"No. In fact, *reliable* communication on 420 megacycles is limited pretty nearly to line of sight. Much greater distances are achieved, of course, under unusual conditions, just as you occasionally get freak TV reception from a station many hundreds of miles away. Taxicab companies operating in the neighboring 460-mc. band have found that with the transmitter feeding an antenna 50' high they can depend upon reaching cabs cruising within a radius of eight to ten miles from the transmitter tower. On the other hand, atmospherics have practically no effect on reception and the wavelength is so short that the signals penetrate into tunnels, bridges, etc."

"What's the short wavelength got to do with that?"

"A scientific description would have to go into the modes of waveguide operation, but let's just say that a radio wave is very much like a cat. You know, they say a cat's whiskers serve it as a sort of feeler gage, and that the cat will not insert its head into any opening that the ends of those whiskers will not clear. A radio wave operates the same way. Unless a tunnel-like passage has cross-sectional dimensions sufficiently great with regard to the wavelength of a radio wave, that wave will not enter the passageway. A good example of this would be when your car radio goes dead inside the framework of an iron bridge. "But I like to fool around with u.h.f. because the field is not as crowded as are the lower frequencies. Here a bright young man like myself—ahem!—just might discover something new all by himself. On top of that, it's a wonderful place to play around with antennas because the half-wave elements are measured in inches instead of feet. You can build an elaborate multi-element array and set it on top of your dining room table. Gene will be using such a collinear array on top of his apartment building, and he has equipped this job with a clever collapsing corner-reflector that folds up and fits inside the case when not being used, but will provide 10-db gain over a simple dipole when opened out."

The boys had been so busy talking that the distance to the hills melted away without their noticing it, and as Jerry finished they found themselves standing in the deep notch cut through the rough limestone where the road went over the small mountain. Hitching up their belts, they started the short but arduous climb to the top of the cut.

"Whew!" Jerry exclaimed as they finally made it. He set the bulky transmitter-receiver case on the ground and stretched out on his back. "A guy ought to drink goat milk before trying that."

"*You* should talk," Carl remarked as he set the heavy battery box squarely on top of his pal's stomach. "How would you like to tote *that* all those seven miles from town?"

Jerry squirmed out from beneath the box and began to open up the portable station case. In just a matter of minutes, he had the connecting cable plugged into the battery case; and the corner reflector, opened up so that it looked like the wide-open jaws of a striking snake, was aimed at the distant town.

"We've got a while to wait," Jerry remarked, as he glanced at his wristwatch. "Gene was not to start looking for us until a half hour from now."

"Where are the earphones?" Carl asked.

"This set uses a speaker, and you'll be surprised at the volume," Jerry told him. "The output stage is operated class B so as to put out a good strong signal and yet be as economical as possible so far as battery current is concerned."

"Let's see now," Carl reflected, "class B tubes are biased so that they draw practically no plate current without a signal on their grids. The plate current rises as there is need for it to handle an increasing signal voltage on the grids. Right?"

"Hundred per cent—" Jerry started to say, when the receiver he was idly tuning blared forth with such a bellow that he fell backward off the rock on which he had been sitting.

"W9CFI! W9CFI! W9CFI! Here is W9HST calling. If you're hearing me, Jerry, come in at once. This is important!"

Jerry scrambled back to his knees, threw a switch and shouted into the mike, "W9HST, W9HST. You're five by nine, Gene. What's up? W9CFI over."

"Roger, Jerry, and listen closely, for we haven't much time. A gang of men just held up the Farmers & Merchants Bank and have headed out that road in your direction. I was down in the police station when the report came in. A couple of carloads of men are after them, but the police chief says they can never catch the hopped-up hot rod the robbers are using before they reach Old Saddle Back. Once across it, the thieves can lose themselves a dozen different ways in the valley on the other side. I told the chief, who is right here with me, that maybe you and Carl could stop them. Do you think you can do it—without getting hurt, I mean? They're bad characters and shot a teller in the bank during the holdup."

As this transmission was coming through, Carl and Jerry stared at each other with widening eyes across the receiver case.

"Stand by while we talk it over," Jerry finally said weakly into the mike, and then his eyes followed Carl's searching stare down into the valley toward town. Because of the trees, the course of the road could only be seen for a short distance, and there was no sign of a car.

"Don't look at me," Carl said to the eyes he could now feel boring into the back of his head. "I promised my mother never to have anything to do with bank robbers."

"We've *got* to do something," Jerry declared, as he rubbed his flat-topped haircut in desperation. "You start pushing rocks down onto the road. Just get enough of them down there, spaced so that a car can't pass through without blowing a tire or knocking a hole in the oil pan. If you can make it look like a rockslide, all the better; but just make sure a car will have to stop until the rocks are cleared away before it can pass."

Without waiting for an answer to this command, he pushed the transmit switch and barked into the mike: "Gene, have the chief get three of his men up there in your shack on the double. Give the chief and each of the men a number from one through four. In a couple of minutes I'll start calling out a number first and then say a short sentence. Have the man whose number is called step up to the mike and repeat that sentence in just as mean and hardboiled a fashion as he can. And you will have to listen closely, for I'll be whispering into the mike—"

He broke off sharply as his straining ears caught the distant throbbing of a racing motor. Instantly he began dragging the portable station case over to the edge of the cut and stopped right at the brink where a small bush hid him from view from below. A glance down at the road revealed that Carl had done an excellent job of blocking it, and now that worthy threw himself, panting heavily, down beside Jerry.

"Help me prop up the back of the case so that the speaker points down at the road," Jerry said; "then, when and if we get the car stopped, you keep moving back and forth just out of sight along the edge of the cut. Try to make a lot of noise. And keep your fingers and toes crossed. We're going to need all the help we can get."

As he finished saying this, a car came roaring over the rise, and then, as the driver glimpsed the rocks in the road, slithered crosswise to a stop amid a great screeching of brakes and showering of gravel.

"What're you stopping for, you fool?" a hawk-nosed man in the rear seat demanded.

"I can't drive over that rockslide," the driver answered sharply.

"Well, all right. Everybody pile out and get those rocks out of the way," Hawknose ordered. "Those yokels back there ain't chasing us to give us the key to the city, you know."

All of the men except Hawknose got out of the car and started toward the pile of rocks. Jerry whispered a few words into the mike and threw the switch to the receive position.

"All right, you birds," a gruff voice bellowed from the speaker; "freeze right where you are. The first one who makes a move gets sprayed with double death from this tommy gun."

The men stopped in their tracks. Only their eyes shifted nervously from one to another and then turned toward the car.

"And you, Bugle Nose, crawl out of that car with your hands over your head or we'll rip it open like a can of sardines," the voice ordered.

The man in the car hesitated, and promptly the harsh voice shouted, "All right, you asked for it; now you're going to get it."

"Hold it! I'm getting out," the man with the large nose said hastily, as he scrambled out the car door with his wrists stretching up out of his coat sleeves.

"That's better," the rasping voice commented. "Bill, you keep a bead right on Bugle Beak's belt buckle and let him have it first if anyone makes a funny move of any kind. Brad, you watch the two on the right."

"Okay, Chief," another voice answered after a little pause.

"Spike, you keep an eye on the other two."

"Gotcha, Chief," was the prompt reply in still a third voice.

"Now let's everyone very, very carefully take his gun out of his pocket and drop it on the road. Then kick it off to one side. If one of you will be so accommodating as to try a little funny stuff, he can save the county the cost of a trial for the whole lot of you."

Like a scene in slow motion, the men began relieving themselves of a collection of revolvers and automatic pistols. It was noteworthy that the .45 automatic of Hawknose was the first to clank on the gravel. Doubtless the mental picture of the submachine gun pointed at his belt buckle had something to do with his alacrity.

After the guns were kicked aside, there was a long pause. Carl, who had been busily scurrying back and forth, dragging his feet and trying to sound like a small posse, looked over his shoulder at Jerry.

That youth's round face was nearly apoplectic as he fiddled desperately with the controls of the u.h.f. station that quite obviously had gone dead. A hurried peek over the edge of the cut revealed that the men below had sensed that something was wrong, and a couple of them were cautiously edging toward their guns.

"What's wrong?" Carl whispered hoarsely, as he bent over his frantically working chum.

"Don't know; but this outfit is as dead as we're going to be in about sixty seconds," Jerry answered.

Spurred on by this electrifying prospect, Carl drew back and made the typical American's classic and ultimate military service gesture for non-operating equipment: he gave the case of the portable station a lusty kick. Instantly Gene's anxious voice burst from the speaker demanding: "What's wrong, Jerry? We can't hear you. What do you want us to do now?"

Before either the bandits or the horrified boys had time to react to this development, another car came over the hill and slid to a stop behind the first. Men erupted from the car into the side ditches in twin sprays the way grasshoppers clear your path in the fall of the year; but before the bandits had time to take advantage of the shock that the unexpected sight of them gave the posse, the latter recovered themselves and collared the unarmed desperadoes. Jerry leaped to his feet and began to shout, "Boys, are we glad to see you—" but as a bullet from the gun of a trigger-happy posse member ricocheted off the rock at his feet and whined off into the distance, he ducked back behind his bush.

"Wouldn't it be too bad if you potted one of your buddies up there!" the hawk-nosed man sneered.

At this moment, the voice of the chief of police bellowed from the speaker. "You men down there listen to me. This is Chief Hall. These two boys up here stopped the bandits and held them for you. Here's the way they did it." And then he went ahead to describe the ruse in detail.

"Finally," he continued, "I'd like to say two things. First, you boys will be in on a nice reward for helping to capture those bandits. Secondly, I don't know what kind of books you've been reading, shows you've been seeing, or TV programs you've been watching, but let me tell you here and now that real cops simply don't talk the way you've just made us talk. We're all going right down to the station and wash our mouths out with soap!"

Jerry and Carl grinned happily at each other as the chief signed off.

"This has certainly taught me one thing," Jerry confessed, beginning to pack up the portable station. "I'll bet that as long as I live I'll never again be careless about inserting a plug in a socket. It was the battery cable plug that caused the set to go dead. I found it while the posse was grabbing those characters down there."

"I give up," Carl said, as he tossed his hands into the air. "A guy who keeps on trouble-shooting when there's a good chance of shooting-trouble is beyond all hope!"   —30—

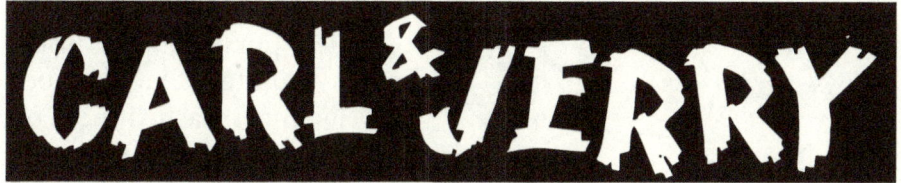

LIE DETECTOR TELLS ALL

November 1955

Jerry stretched out on the worn old-leather-covered couch in his basement laboratory, was jerked out of his pleasant reverie by the banging of the cellar door against the wall as his chum and neighbor, Carl Anderson, came striding in.

"Hey, Jer, how do you give artificial respiration to a night crawler?" Carl asked excitedly as he dangled a very limp worm, a full ten inches long, directly in front of Jerry's crossing eyes.

"Get that young snake out of my face," Jerry commanded as he struggled to a sitting position; "and what kind of a stupid question is *that*?"

"It's *not* stupid," Carl denied heatedly. "If we can just bring Old Droopy here and his buddies back to life, we're on our way to being millionaires!"

"Again?" Jerry said languidly as he smothered a yawn. "Let's hear your latest lid-flipper."

"On their drive last Sunday, my folks gathered up a couple of bushels of walnuts along the road," Carl explained. "I have to hull them by driving them through a knothole in a board. As you know, this is a messy business; so to avoid getting any more of that sticky, staining walnut hull juice on me than necessary, I decided to run water over the crate of nuts before starting. The water filtered down through them and spread over the ground. In nothing flat, worms started wriggling up out of the wet earth. Apparently that walnut hull juice gave them a real hotfoot, for they were in such a hurry to get away from it that they popped to the surface and practically stood on their tails.

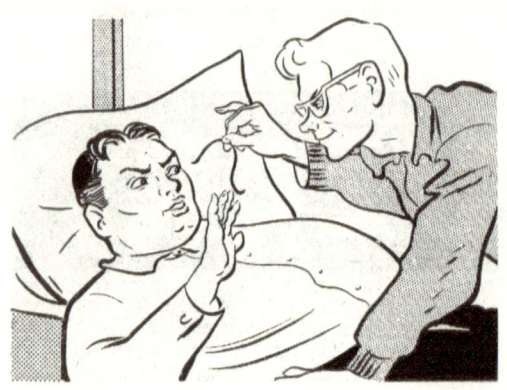

"I grabbed them faster than a woman snatching up the contents of her spilled purse, but in just a few minutes they stopped wriggling. I washed them off in clear water and even tried brushing Droopy here with some of Mom's super-gentle soap powder, but he refuses to come around. I figure artificial respiration is the last hope; if you will just point out where his ribs are so I'll know where to put my thumbs, we'll get started. If we can revive him, we're in business. We can grind up the walnut hulls and sell a small vial of the powder for a dollar. The purchaser need only mix a few gallons of water with this powder and pour the solution on the ground. After a few minutes, he can pick up a couple of cans of fish worms and be on his way. Think of it: no strain, no pain, and no spading!"

"Well," Jerry commented, as he gingerly prodded the worm Carl had placed on the couch beside him with his forefinger, "all I can suggest is that you include a bottle of embalming fluid with every vial of that walnut hull powder. That's the only thing that will 'save' Droopy now. How come you're all at once money-mad, anyway?"

"I've decided we need an oscilloscope for our laboratory," Carl announced importantly. "After boning up on this instrument, I'm convinced there are any number of interesting experiments and important tests that can be made with it. What's more, it would come in mighty handy for checking my transmitter, especially now that I'm starting to build a single-sideband suppressed-carrier job. We can buy a scope kit that will fill our needs nicely for around fifty dollars, but first we've got to latch on to the fifty."

"I commend your ambition, but I decry your methods," Jerry announced pompously. "You must learn to think electronically. If we need new electronic equipment, let's make the electronic equipment and know-how we already have pay for it."

"Such as how?" Carl demanded.

"It's all arranged," Jerry said, with elaborate casualness. "The Acme TV Service Shop is opening this weekend and holding open house on both Friday and Saturday. I talked the guy who owns it into a big deal of letting me set up a lie detector there in the store and give free lie-detector tests to anyone who wants to try it. He figures this will be just the unusual type of gimmick to draw a crowd; he'll pay me 25 bucks for giving tests Friday night and all day Saturday."

"Oh, fine! Now all you gotta do is buy a lie detector!"

"No such thing. Back in May, 1955, *Popular Electronics* published an article on how to make a gadget to use with your v.t.v.m. to serve as a lie detector. This is a simple little gadget; and all the parts for it, except the tube and B battery, came out of our junk box. I 'borrowed' these other two items from Dad's portable radio that he won't be using—I hope—until next spring. Come on over to the bench, and I'll show you how it works.

Just then, however, Mr. and Mrs. Bishop, Jerry's parents, came in through the inside door leading to the basement storage room. Mrs. Bishop had a bushel basket, and Mr. Bishop carried a spading fork and had the unhappy look of a man reluctantly being prodded into digging up flower bulbs for winter storage.

"Well, well, what are our young inventors up to now?" he questioned, with the hysterical joviality of a man snatching at straws to put off the start of an unpleasant job.

"I was just going to show Carl how my new lie detector works," Jerry explained.

"Show me!" Mr. Bishop insisted. "I always did want to see if those things really could tell when an iron-nerved man like myself chose to toy with the truth."

"Well, all right," Jerry agreed. "Just slip these two metal thimbles with the wires attached over the middle fingers on each hand. They are the connecting electrodes that enable the instrument to measure any change in the resistance path between them. When you're emotionally disturbed, as you will be if you try to avoid the truth, the change in your body resistance will be indicated by the swing of this meter pointer on the vacuum-tube voltmeter."

With an amused smile, Mr. Bishop slipped the electrodes on his

finger tips and watched his son balance the bridge circuit so that the meter pointer rested in the left-hand portion of the scale.

"What is your name?" Jerry asked.

"Milton Bishop."

"Where do you live?"

"1810 Spear Street."

"What do you work at?"

"I'm an architect."

Mrs. Bishop, who had been impatiently watching the quiet needle of the v.t.v.m., broke in with: "Let my try. You told me you couldn't come home for dinner last night because you had to work late at the office. Is that true?"

"Certainly," was Mr. Bishop's prompt reply as he turned to smile fondly at his wife. For a split second nothing happened, and then the meter started to climb. As it reached full-scale, Mr. Bishop turned harriedly from the accusing meter to the still more accusing eyes of his wife.

"I *did* work late, a whole half hour," he insisted; "then a bunch of us fellows went over to Vic Cline's to see his new twenty-five horsepower outboard motor. A little game started somehow . . . and the time sort of got away from us . . ."

As his voice trailed off in this weak explanation, he jerked off the thimbles as though they were red-hot and flung them down on the bench.

"Well, come on, Iron Nerves, let's make with the spading fork," Mrs. Bishop suggested with a mocking, victorious smile.

"Oh, no, you don't!" her husband exclaimed. "Let's see you try the lie detector, Mabel."

In spite of her protests, Mr. Bishop slipped the thimbles on her fingers and watched impatiently while Jerry rebalanced the bridge circuit.

"Your name, Madam?" Mr. Bishop snapped.

"Mabel Bishop."

"Your age?"

"Thirty-seven—no, I mean thirty-eight," Mrs. Bishop hurriedly amended, as the meter pointer began a threatening upward movement.

"Just a few minutes ago I noticed a long scratch on the right rear fender of the car. Would you know anything about that?"

"I was intending to mention that to you," Mrs. Bishop began calmly. "It must have happened in the supermarket parking lot. I didn't notice it until I came home ... or at least I don't remember noticing it ... or if I did I forgot about it ... or maybe I do remember hearing a little noise as I was backing out of the garage ..."

She kept talking more and more frantically in her effort to stop the relentless march of the meter pointer up-scale, but it was no use. In spite of Jerry's repeated rebalancing of the bridge, the pointer kept crawling up.

"I thought so!" Mr. Bishop gloated. "For your information, that scratch is just level with the hasp on the door frame."

"Maybe we had better go and dig those bulbs now," Mrs. Bishop remarked quietly, as she removed the thimbles and placed them gently on the bench. Obediently, but with a smirk still on his face, Mr. Bishop followed her outside.

"Boy, that thing really works!" Carl said enthusiastically, as Jerry's parents closed the door behind them.

"Yes," Jerry agreed, as he slipped on the thimbles and rebalanced the instrument; "it's an interesting little device. Of course a 'polygraph,' as a laboratory-type lie detector is called, is quite a bit more complicated than this. It records the reaction of the person being examined to each question by means of scribing pens tracing on moving sheets of paper; and sometimes the pulse rate, respiration, and other factors are recorded as well as the skin resistance; but for our purposes—"

He turned around as he heard the outside door quietly open to admit his father.

"I'm supposed to be after another basket," Mr. Bishop announced in a hushed conspiratorial voice; "but I wanted to have a word with you two about that lie detector you've built up. A man isn't safe with a vacuum tube snitcher like that lying around. We men know that a little white lie is necessary now and then; so that thing has gotta go. What will you take to dismantle the gadget? Ten dollars?"

"Well, I don't know," Jerry said hesitantly. "After all, there is a considerable investment in parts—" Quickly, but unobtrusively, he wriggled his fingers out of the thimbles as the tell-tale meter pointer started upward.

"Okay, I'll make it fifteen dollars," Mr. Bishop said hurriedly, as he took out his wallet; "but remember that this is just between us men. Not a word to your mother."

He got another basket, shot a baleful glance at the lie detector resting on the bench, and went outside again. He had barely closed the door behind him when Mrs. Bishop opened the other door.

"I was just looking for your father," she remarked casually, as she sat down on the couch from which Carl thoughtfully snatched the carcass of Old Droopy before she noticed it. "I believe I'll rest a bit, though, if you boys don't mind."

"Sure, Mom; glad to have you," Jerry said.

"You know," she commenced, in a very offhand manner, "I've been thinking about that amusing little toy you have built up; and I'm not at all sure you boys should be playing with such a thing. While we know it is just a plaything, an electronic tattletale like that *could* cause trouble. In fact, I'm afraid that it has already embarrassed your poor father; and we can't have that, now, can we? If you'll tear it up, I think I might be able to give you, say, ten dollars, to buy something really worth while for your laboratory."

"Gee, Mom, that's swell of you; and we'll certainly tear up the silly thing the first of next week," Jerry promised.

She reached into her apron pocket and handed over a ten-dollar bill, then went out in search of Mr. Bishop.

"Why didn't you hold out for fifteen dollars, the way you did with your Dad?" Carl demanded.

"You don't haggle with ladies," Jerry explained chivalrously, "and anyway, the twenty-five they gave us plus the twenty-five we'll get from Acme TV Service will just buy that new scope kit. There's no use in being a hog about things."

"Guess you're right," Carl agreed, "and I've got to take off my hat to you. When it comes to harvesting the old government lettuce, electronics has fish worms beat all to heck!"   —30—

SANTA'S LITTLE HELPERS

December 1955

The cozy warmth of the basement laboratory felt good to Carl as he stepped in out of the crisp December weather. He removed his steaming glasses and peered owlishly at his buddy Jerry, sitting at the workbench busily engaged in doing something with a large box of dial lamp bulbs, several short lengths of insulated flexible wire, some little jars of colored liquid, and a soldering iron.

"What're you up to?" Carl demanded. "Getting homesick for the June fireflies and trying to make up some synthetic ones?"

"That's not too far off," Jerry grunted, without looking up. "I'm cooking up some miniature Christmas tree lights for our tree."

"How?" Carl asked.

"Well, what I'm really doing is connecting 20 of these No. 40 panel lamps in a series string to be connected across the light line. That way, the 120 volts in the line divides up so that each bulb has six volts across it. Since the bulbs are rated at from 6 to 8 volts, this should allow them to operate for a long time without burning out. I could just as well have used No. 47 bulbs, which are identical electrically but have bayonet instead of screw bases. However, I was able to buy this large box of No. 40's at a bargain. For that matter, No. 44 bulbs could also have been used to get a little more light; but since they draw 250 milliamperes of current instead of the 150 ma. drawn by the No. 40's and get quite a bit hotter, the lower-current bulbs will be safer to use."

"Since No. 40's and No. 47's draw the same current, you could mix them in the same string; but No. 44's could not be mixed with either of the other two types. Check?"

"Check," Jerry nodded.

"How far apart will the bulbs be?"

"A foot and a half. That's why I'm cutting these 18" lengths of wire, stripping about ⅛" of insulation off both ends, and then tinning the ends. When this is done, I'll simply solder a tinned wire end to the tip of one of the bulbs with the wire pointing straight down away from the bulb; on the other end of this wire, I'll solder the screw base of a second bulb with the glass bulb pointing away from the wire. A second wire will be soldered to the tip of the second bulb and dressed parallel to the other wire. The base of a third bulb, lying next to the first bulb, will be soldered to the free end of this last wire, and so on. When I get through, I'll have a row of ten bulbs at the top and ten bulbs at the bottom all neatly connected in series by zigzag lengths of wire. Two longer lengths of wire can be run from an a.c. plug to the base of the first bulb and the tip of the last one to make the string ready to be connected to the line."

"You're not going to leave those 'hot' connections exposed, I hope," Carl said with a quick frown.

"Well, hardly! Each bulb base will be completely covered with a neat wrapping of this thin plastic tape that extends from well up on the glass to down below the tip and holds the two wire leads firmly together. The tape adds very little bulk, really sticks, and is rated at several thousand volts of insulation."

"Won't clear bulbs look kind of monotonous?"

"They're not going to be clear. That's why I bought this dial lamp coloring kit. It has little jars of liquid red, green, blue, and amber coloring material as well as a jar of solvent. All I have to do is dip a bulb in the proper coloring solution, and presto, I have a red, a green, a blue, or an amber colored bulb. If I get tired of one color, I can use the solvent to remove it and start all over. I think I'll make up several strings and dip all the bulbs of one string in the same color. After all, a whole string draws less than 20 watts, so power consumption is no item. Just once I'd like to see a tree really full of colored lights."

"Are you just dreaming about how these lights will look or have you seen such trees?"

"I've seen them. John Crump, who works in the engineering department of the *RMB Company,* has been using strings like these for five years, and they really look swell. It's surprising how much light those little bulbs throw; yet they're small enough so that they really *decorate* a tree instead of covering it up. What's more, they are the easiest things in the world to put on the tree or take off. They are so light that they can be put on the tips of the smallest branches."

"How about burn outs? Replacing a bulb would require unwrapping the tape, unsoldering the wires, and soldering in a new bulb. You could, of course, locate a burned-out bulb with a pair of insulation-piercing probes and an ohmmeter; but it seems to me that would be a good bit of trouble if these bulbs burn out as fast as the common series-string type do."

"That's the good part: They don't. John tells me he has been using the same half-dozen strings for five years, and not a single bulb has conked out in all that time. He mentioned one rather funny thing, though. He says the bulbs colored blue get noticeably hotter than those colored red or amber. We decided that the blue coloring doesn't transmit the heat radiated by the filament as well as the red and amber coloring does."

"Okay, I'm sold, and you're a genius," Carl exclaimed. "How's about helping me with *my* Christmas problem? Two years ago Dad and I built a life-size Santa and put it out in the front yard. The eyes of Santa lighted up whenever he was awake—which oddly enough was just about time the little kids came past on the way home from school—and they thought he was real cool. Last year I put an intercom unit in Old Nick's tummy, and he was even more popular because he could listen and talk back, although I'm afraid his 'ho-ho-hoing' was a bit on the treble side. This year I've got to come up with something new. Modern kids demand constant progress, and unless Santa has learned some new tricks since last Christmas, they're going to think the old boy is pretty stupid."

"Hm-m-m, we should be able to dream up something," Jerry murmured slowly as he closed his eyes to think better. "I think I've got it! Use extension cords to put the mike of the tape recorder and a small speaker connected to its external speaker jack inside Santa along with the intercom unit. Then you can use the intercom to persuade each

kid to tell Old Santa what he wants for Christmas. As he starts to talk, you take down the list on tape."

"I'm with you so far. Go on."

"Well, you could put out a spiel to the effect that Old Santa wants to be real sure he remembers the list of each kid. Since he is really modern, he has worked out a system whereby he quick-freezes the words of the child as he hears them and then stores the frozen messages away in his ice-chest until he is ready to pack his bag for the Christmas Eve trip. If any child doubts all this, Santa will be quite willing to take the frozen message out of the ice-chest and thaw it out so the child can hear his own voice giving the list—over the speaker connected to the tape recorder, naturally. You'll need a couple of sound effects to go along with this business. There should be some sort of tinkling sound to accompany the 'freezing' of the messages, and then there ought to be a sizzling sputtering sound when they are being 'thawed out'."

"Now, wait just a little minute. You know as well as I do how hard it is to locate a short recorded, section on a tape when you're in a hurry. By the time I found a particular message and thawed it out, the kid himself would be frozen in his tracks waiting to hear it."

"I've thought of that, too. Don't try to record all the messages on one long roll of tape. Instead, cut up a roll of inexpensive tape into

5' lengths and hang them neatly over a tie rack. Then, when a child wants to tell Santa all about it, you simply thread the end of one of these tapes into the recording slot and between the pressure rollers. While you are recording, the tape will simply feed through and either bunch up on top of the recorder or slide off on the floor. Five feet of tape at 3¾ inches per second will give each kid about 15 seconds to make his wants known—which is plenty long enough unless his parents are richer than yours and mine are. As the recording is finished, write the child's name on the back of the leading end with a china marking pencil and hang it up so his name can be easily read. Then, when any moppet wants proof that his message to Santa is still safely on file, you can pick out the proper tape quickly and start it through the recorder."

"What a brain!" Carl exclaimed admiringly, as he roughly brushed Jerry's flat-top haircut. "And I've got a little scheme of my own. After Christmas is over, we can take those recordings and have them rerecorded on small disc records and sell them at a good profit to the parents of the children as keepsakes."

"We *could,* but I'm sort of agin it," Jerry said slowly. "Maybe the old Christmas spirit has got me, but somehow I don't want any part of commercializing Christmas any more than it is. If any parents want to have recordings made at their own cost, that would be quite all right; but let us just take our reward in the form of the fun we'll have amusing the children."

"Right!" Carl quickly agreed, "and I'm a little ashamed that I even thought of it."   —30—

TRAPPED IN A CHIMNEY

January 1956

"Man, did you ever see a sweeter flying job?" Carl demanded enthusiastically, as he and his chum, Jerry, squinted at Carl's radio-controlled model plane sailing along against the late afternoon January sky.

"Surely does handle well," Jerry agreed, doing a little jig on the frozen ground to keep warm. It had been a fine winter day with the temperature up in the 40's, but now the mercury was sinking with the sun. The boys were flying their model in a large field just beyond the outskirts of town. At the other end of the field were the ruins of a box factory that had been completely destroyed by fire several years before. Only a tall brick chimney had been left standing.

"Better bring it in for a landing," Jerry suggested. "It's getting late, and I think I can smell snow in the air."

"Okey-dokey," Carl agreed; "but get a load of this tight turn around that smokestack."

As he said this, he stuck his finger in the opening marked "L. Trn." of the telephone dial mounted on the transmitter control box, pulled it down against the stop and released it. Instantly the little plane banked gracefully and turned toward the top of the smokestack.

"Hey!" yelled Jerry, whose depth perception was much better than Carl's, "you've turned too quick!"

By the time he got the warning out, however, and in spite of all the "body English" he tried to put on the little plane, it closed the gap between it and the smokestack—and failed to appear on the other side. At the same instant, the steady snarl of the little motor ceased abruptly.

"Holy cow!" Carl groaned, "it's crashed!"

He set the control box on the ground and started at a dead run across the field. Jerry followed, but Carl's long legs and athletic build gave him such an advantage that by the time his chubby companion came puffing up to the base of the chimney Carl had loped around it twice.

"Hey, that's funny," Carl muttered. "I can't see a thing of it, and there's no place for it to hide, unless—" As though worked by a common string, the heads of both boys tilted back as they stared up at the top of the chimney towering some sixty or seventy feet above them.

"That's where it went," Jerry said with conviction. "It was just skimming the top, and I thought it might clear; but it must have dived right into the top. Well, scratch one model plane."

"That's what *you* think," Carl said determinedly, reaching for a rung of the wide ladder going up the side of the chimney. "I've got at least a gallon of sweat and several acres of lawn mowing invested in that gas motor and the plane controls, and I intend to get 'em back or know the reason why."

"All right," Jerry said resignedly, as he started up the ladder behind his friend; "I'm just stupid enough to go along with you."

In a few minutes, the boys were standing side by side on an upper rung of the ladder while they leaned over the broad lip of the smokestack opening and stared down its throat. Even at the narrowed top, the stack measured a good eight feet across.

"Heck," Carl said in disappointment, "it's too dark down there to see a thing."

"Hold your horses a minute," Jerry grunted, as he squirmed around on his stomach so that he could reach into a pocket and pull out the flashlight case that contained the booster-battery used in starting the plane motor. He unscrewed the adapter with its two flexible leads from the bulb socket, screwed the bulb back in place, and replaced the lens cap. When the restored flashlight was shone down into the chimney, the white cross formed by the wing and fuselage of the plane could be faintly seen at the bottom.

"You hold the flashlight. I'm going down and get it," Carl announced.

"Oh, no, you don't," Jerry exclaimed, as he threw a fat leg over the edge of the stack and reached for the top rung of the rusty narrow iron ladder that went down the inside of the chimney. "This is my chance to check up on that old business about whether or not you can see stars in daytime from the bottom of a well or chimney, and I'm not going to muff it. You can tag along if you want to."

Cautiously, the two boys went down the rust-eaten ladder. All went well until they were about ten feet from the bottom, and then suddenly the whole lower section of the ladder gave way under their combined weight and they dropped to the bottom of the chimney. Jerry fell on his back on the layer of soft ashes at the bottom of the chimney, and Carl came down on top of him. The section of ladder broke into several pieces and clattered harmlessly around them. Carl quickly sprang to his feet and looked anxiously down at his friend still lying on his back and staring intently up at the little circle of blue far above them.

"Are you hurt, Jerry? Can't you get up?"

"You *can* see stars, and they're all different colors," Jerry observed softly, in a bemused voice.

"Come on; snap out of it," Carl said, unceremoniously yanking Jerry to his feet. "You don't need to go down a chimney to see the kind of stars you're seeing. Hey! Did you *have* to light squarely on top of my plane?"

"There's just no pleasing some people," Jerry sighed, as he lifted the flattened model from where he had been lying and shook the ashes from it. "Here I break your fall with my very own body, and all you do is gripe about your darn plane. I think we're mighty fortunate. If that ladder had broken loose a little farther up, we'd both have been killed;

and it would have been our own stupid fault. Trusting that rickety old iron ladder was not one of our brighter acts."

"You can say that again," Carl agreed, as he stared owlishly about him in the dim light that filtered down from above; "but now the $64,000 question is: how are we going to get out of here? There's nothing to climb on to reach the bottom end of that ladder, and I wouldn't want to trust it again if we could reach it. These chimney walls are too thick to chisel through even if we had tools. The one opening through the wall, that one up there near the bottom end of the ladder where the smoke from the boilers came in, is sealed off solidly with heavy metal plates that sagged down over it when the box factory burned. I've noticed that before from the outside."

"If you were Tarzan, you might go hand over hand up this little cable that runs along the side of the chimney," Jerry observed. "What's it for, anyway?"

"It's a ground lead for the lightning rods on the top," Carl said; "but I'm not Tarzan, and I wouldn't want to trust my weight on it if I were. No, I'm beginning to think we'll never get out of here without help. We've got to cook up some way to let people know we're in here."

"Like yelling?"

"A fat lot of good that'll do. We never saw a soul around here all afternoon; and now that it's getting dark, no one will be around for sure."

"We might build a fire. Then when people saw the smoke, they'd come to investigate."

"A dandy idea *if* we had something to burn, *if* people could see smoke in the dark, and *if* we didn't suffocate long before anyone noticed the imaginary smoke."

"Okay, smarty; you make some suggestions and let me knock them in the head for a while."

"Let's see what we've got in our pockets. Maybe that will give us an idea. All I've got in mine is a cigarette lighter, a dime, a quarter, and this little piece of wire."

"I can do better than that," Jerry boasted. "I've got this flashlight and the booster-battery adapter. Here's a small file I brought along to dress that nick out of the propeller blade. Finally, here's one slightly squashed chocolate bar that was in my hip pocket. We had better cut that up in small portions and eat just a little bit each day to keep up our strength."

"That's out," Carl said flatly. "If we don't get out of here pretty soon, we'll freeze to death anyway; so let's break that in two and eat it right away. Maybe it will help us think. All I can think of right now is that Mom is having spaghetti and meatballs for supper tonight, and there's going to be an empty chair at the supper table."

For a little while, the two friends munched their chocolate in silence. Finally Jerry said slowly: "What we really need is some way to send out a call for help. If you had just brought that control transmitter with you, we might have been able to rig up some sort of low-frequency transmitter with the parts, but we surely can't build a transmitter with what we've got here. We don't even have a tube."

"They had transmitters before there were tubes," Carl pointed out. "Don't forget the old spark coil jobs. But that doesn't help either because we don't have any spark coil—"

He broke off abruptly as Jerry leaped to his feet and snatched the broken model plane from the ground.

"Who says we don't?" Jerry gloated, starting to remove the tiny induction coil from the fuselage. "This thing makes a spark for the motor, and it will make a spark for a transmitter."

"This I gotta see," Carl said dubiously. "You've got to have either a.c. or rapidly pulsating d.c. in the primary of that coil to get a continuous spark discharge across the secondary. Where are you going to get that?"

"Fire up that lighter of yours, and just watch and see," Jerry said, as he busied himself with the coil and the booster-battery adapter for the flashlight.

In a few minutes, Jerry had a haywire arrangement of wires, flashlight case, and induction coil spread out on the ashy floor. Two bits of the wire from Carl's pocket had been used to form a small spark gap across the secondary of the induction coil. One terminal of the flashlight battery was connected to one end of the induction coil primary, but leads from the other side of the battery and the other side of the primary were left free.

At Jerry's direction, Carl used the rest of the wire to connect one side of the spark gap to the lightning arrester cable. The other side he stuck in the ground several feet away. Finally, Jerry connected one of the loose primary wires to the blade of the file and pressed the end of the other wire against Carl's quarter. When the quarter was drawn rapidly across the serrations of the file, the rapid making and breaking of the primary circuit of the induction coil produced a ragged blue spark discharge across the small gap.

"It works!" Jerry exclaimed. "What shall I say? Had we better start out with SOS or use the amateur emergency call, QRR?"

"Better use SOS," Carl advised as the lighter flickered out. "More people are familiar with that. Then go ahead and say something like, 'Please send help to the old box factory chimney. We are imprisoned within it and—'"

"All right, Charles Dickens; cut it short," Jerry interrupted. "This quarter-and-file keying arrangement is not exactly a bug, you know. I'm going to send 'SOS box factory stack' over and over and let 'em take it from there."

With this, he started drawing the coin across the file in short and long strokes to form the respective dots and dashes. "Z-z, z-z, z-z; z-z-z-z, z-z-z-z-z, z-z-z-z-z; z-z, z-z, z-z," hissed the little spark, and its light cast a flashing, eerie, blue glow on the intent faces of the two boys. By now it was almost completely dark inside the chimney, and Jerry "keyed" the transmitter entirely by sense of touch. Needless to say, the sending was not exactly machine-like.

After a quarter of an hour or so, the batteries grew so weak that the spark would no longer jump the gap. The bits of wire were pushed closer together and the message repeated until even this smaller gap was too much for the failing batteries.

"That's it, I guess," Jerry announced. "After resting a few hours, the batteries will recover enough to let us make one more short transmission; we'll save that for daylight."

"What frequency do you suppose we're sending on?"

"Just about all frequencies. A spark gap emits a very broad band of frequencies, and there are no tuned circuits in this rig to peak it up."

"Well," Carl said disconsolately, "it looks like nobody heard it anyway—"

"Listen!" Jerry interrupted. Faintly, but unmistakably, there came the sound of a wailing police siren. It came closer and closer and then stopped abruptly. A few minutes later, the boys heard muffled voices outside the chimney.

"Help! Help! Here in the chimney!" they shouted in unison.

Seconds later, a strong spotlight was shone into their upturned faces from the top of the chimney, and a dangling rope was let down to them. By means of this rope, the boys were hoisted up one at a time until they could reach the bottom end of the broken ladder, and then were helped on up and out of the chimney.

"I might know it would be you two," the police sergeant said coldly, as he surveyed the begrimed but happy boys. "Every time something weird happens in this town, you jokers are mixed up in it."

"Who picked up our message?" Jerry asked eagerly.

"Who didn't!" the sergeant growled. "For the past half hour they've been ringing the police station phone off the wall. A few of the calls were from hams, Boy Scouts, and ex-Army or -Navy operators who actually picked up the message on the broadcast or short-wave bands; but dozens of calls were from irate TV viewers who were just plain mad because someone was clobbering Milton Berle on their sets—and on the very night when Marilyn Monroe was a guest star, too. Right now, you two are probably the most hated pair in this whole town!" —30—

CARL & JERRY

HOW TO HAUNT A HOUSE

February 1956

Bright moonlight bathing the snow-covered landscape made it unnecessary for the two boys to use their flashlights as they trudged up the narrow lane toward the dark and brooding silhouette of the house set well back from the highway. The only sound was that of the snow squeaking beneath their Arctic boots, until the tall one carrying the tape recorder turned his head so that the moonlight glinted on his horn-rimmed glasses as he addressed his short and puffing companion:

"Jer, I'm still a little foggy on why Mr. Arnold is paying us twenty-five dollars, plus cost of equipment, to 'haunt' this old house."

"He wants to get even with a couple of favorite tomboy nieces who really gave him a hard time when he visited them in Florida last spring, Carl. He says that as soon as those two found out he was afraid of bugs and reptiles they really gave him the business. They chased him around the house with a hairy-legged spider that he swears could straddle the mouth of a teacup; they put little chameleon lizards in his bed; and finally, after they had coaxed him to go swimming with them in a little lake near Orlando, one distracted his attention by taking his picture with a movie camera while the other swam under water and clamped a couple of barrel staves around his leg just as the one with the camera shouted, 'Alligator! Alligator.' He vows he could feel teeth in those barrel staves, and he practically splashed the lake dry getting to the bank as the whole thing was recorded on film."

"Say, those two sound like interesting chicks," Carl said admiringly.

"Not really. They're practically old women. One is nineteen, and the other is at least twenty-two," Jerry said disparagingly. "Anyway, they're here visiting the Arnolds, and Mr. Arnold is going to 'con' them into betting they can spend tomorrow night in this old 'haunted house' on his farm without seeing any ghosts. He's run a couple of light wires through the grove that separates this old house from his home so that we can have light down in that hidden cellar room and power to operate the house-haunting gadgets that we installed yesterday afternoon. Tonight we'll check our whole installation to make sure everything works. Mr. Arnold is going to sneak off and meet us if he can get away."

As Jerry finished speaking, they reached the old house and carefully picked their way across the rotting porch to the deeply shadowed front door. "This place looks a heck of a lot different at night than it does in daytime," Carl muttered. "If you ask me, 'spooking' this place is sort of like gilding the lily. I'd not be surprised if there *were* ghosts in there."

"None of that," Jerry said briskly. "As a young scientist, you can only believe in the ghosts you see on your TV screen when an airplane flies over. Shine your flashlight on this keyhole while I—"

He stopped speaking abruptly, and stumbled backward into Carl as the door suddenly swung open with a loud screeching of rusty hinges.

"What do you know! We must not have locked it yesterday afternoon," Jerry exclaimed, as he stepped cautiously inside and probed the corners of the large, nearly empty room with his flashlight. "Now I know how the girls will feel when we *make* the door do that for them tomorrow night."

"How do we work this again?"

"The closed door compresses a little spring in the casing up at the top. Throwing a switch in the cellar allows current to flow through the coil of a solenoid mounted in the door casing by the latch. The magnetic field pulls a spring-loaded soft iron plunger down into the coil. This plunger has an extension sticking out the end of the coil so that its movement, produced by the magnetic field, can exert either a pulling or pushing action. In this case, it pushes back the catch, allowing the compressed spring at the top of the casing to shove the door open as if it had been opened by unseen hands," Jerry explained, as he closed the door and tugged at the knob to make sure that it was securely latched. "Hey," he exclaimed to Carl, "quit walking on my heels and breathing on the back of my neck, will you?"

"This place gives me the creeps tonight," Carl admitted in a half-whisper, as he nervously twitched the beam of his flashlight over the dusty floor, the cracked and cobwebbed windows, the peeling wallpaper, and the warped and sagging open staircase.

"You're just letting your imagination run away with you," Jerry said firmly. "Apparently Mr. Arnold couldn't get away; so we may as well get started. You stay here and observe while I go down in the cellar and operate things. Try to imagine you're seeing what goes on through the eyes of a frightened girl."

"That 'frightened' part will be easy," Carl said through teeth kept tightly closed to prevent their chattering. "What all are you going to do?"

"First I'll make the door come open. Then I'll turn the knob on that multiple-contact wafer switch so that it activates, one after another, the solenoids fastened to the bottom of the stair treads. As the rubber-covered ends of the solenoid plungers bump their respective steps, it should sound very much as if an unseen person were walking up the stairs."

"Then what?"

"Next I'll make this rocking chair rock all by itself," Jerry said, as he carefully checked he position of the old-fashioned chair. "By sending pulses of current through the coil of the electromagnet mounted just below the surface of the floor, I'll give magnetic tugs to the piece of soft iron concealed in the chair rocker just ahead of the point where its curve now contacts the floor. Timing the pulses of current properly should make the chair rock harder and harder. And all this time I'll be working the solenoids we have hidden under he floor and in the walls and ceiling so as to produce a wide variety of plain and fancy 'spiritual knocking.'"

"Remembering how we mounted this stuff and ran wires to it, I'm glad Mr. Arnold intends to tear down this old house in the spring," Carl said.

"That's right. Having his permission to saw and bore and chisel wherever we pleased made things a lot easier. Now, after the chair-rocking act, I'll run the tape recorder into the concealed speakers and play some of those spooky recordings we made of chains rattling, rats squeaking, and hollow groans."

"My favorite is that echoing-crazy-laughter recording we made in the empty main hall of the fair grounds last Sunday afternoon," Carl remarked.

"That *is* a doozy," Jerry agreed. "First I'll play it through the speaker in the back bedroom upstairs, then I'll move it into the speaker at the head of the stairs, and finally I'll feed the recording into one of the speakers in this room. That ought to give the impression of the madman moving in on you. And don't forget, I'll be able to switch any of those speakers into the input of our intercom unit so that they'll serve as microphones and let me hear what's going on in any part of the house. You can keep in touch with me all the time through them. Well, here I go."

Carl stood in the middle of the empty room and watched the rotund figure of his chum move off down the hall with the tape recorder, preceded by the bobbing pool of light furnished by the flashlight. It seemed that this had scarcely disappeared from view when Carl felt a cold draught on the back of his neck and turned around to see the door swinging open to the sound of its grating hinges.

"Man, you surely got things warmed up in a hurry," Carl said nervously, as he closed the door with a bang. "You can check off the door business as operating perfectly. . . . You hear me, Jer?" he called anxiously, after waiting several seconds for an answer that did not come.

"What are you babbling about?" Jerry's voice suddenly boomed from the ceiling. "Just as the intercom warmed up, I heard you say something about the door's working all right, but I haven't even tried it yet. If you're ready, I'll try it now."

"Somebody or *something* beat you to it!" Carl said hoarsely, "but go ahead."

As he said this, the door once more swung open with its "Inner Sanctum" sound effect.

"You don't need to tell me it worked," Jerry called cheerfully. "I could hear it. Now let's walk the ghost up the stairs."

Immediately there was a muffled thump at the bottom of the stairs; then came another and another and another, each sound emanating from a higher step. The sound was so much like that of the footsteps of a heavy man climbing the stairs that Carl imagined he could see a ghostly figure ascending the worn steps. Suddenly the sound stopped for a few seconds; and then, as Jerry started turning the switch knob backwards a position at a time, the sounds started all over again; but this time the ghostly feet were coming *down* the stairs, toward Carl!

"Stop it!" Carl called sharply in a shrill voice. "That's a little *too* realistic."

"Fine, fine!" Jerry's voice came from the speaker concealed in the ceiling. "Now watch the rocking chair. I think I can time the switching by the sound of the rocker if you don't QRM me with those knocking knees of yours."

As if by magic, the rocking chair began swaying back and forth, gently at first and then harder and harder. As Carl stared in fascination at the chair rocking crazily away in the circle of light from his flashlight, it looked exactly as though some ghostly sitter were vigorously entertaining itself.

All at once the whole empty house was filled with a cacophony of discordant sound. From somewhere upstairs there was the clanking of chains mixed in with the high-pitched squeaking of bats. A hollow, echoing laugh rolled down the open stairway. And once more the door swung open and added its rasping groan to the other sounds. Ghostly rappings ran over the walls, ceiling, and floor. As the door came to a stop, wide open, revealing the moonlit snow scene outside, all of the sounds came to an abrupt halt that left the echoes still bouncing off the bare walls. The rocking chair teetered back and forth in a lessening arc.

"Quit opening the door; it's getting cold in here," Carl shouted at the ceiling.

"Who's opening the door?" Jerry demanded. "I haven't touched that switch but once since I came down here."

He broke off as a deep bass chuckle suddenly swelled through the house.

"I didn't know you had a recording like that," Carl said with surprise.

"I haven't," Jerry finally said, in a small scared voice. "That didn't come from me."

All at once the rocking chair began to rock again, wilder than before.

"Are you rocking the chair?" Carl asked in a croaking voice.

"No. I've pulled out all the plugs except that of the intercom unit. Something odd is going on. I'm coming up."

In nothing flat, Jerry came charging down the hall, and the two boys huddled together at one end of the room and watched the chair swaying crazily back and forth, back and forth, back and forth.

"I'm getting out of here," Carl shouted as he bolted for the door, with Jerry right at his heels.

"Wait, boys!" the deep bass voice boomed from upstairs. Carl stopped in the open doorway, and the two boys shined their flashlights up the staircase. There at the top loomed a familiar laughing figure.

"It's Mr. Arnold!" Jerry exclaimed.

"That's right," Mr. Arnold said as he came down the creaking steps, still chuckling aloud. "I hope you boys won't hold it against me, but I simply *had* to find out how effective the little entertainment we have planned for my smart-aleck nieces is going to be. If I could scare you two with your own electronic goblins, I knew that we would have a sure-fire bet to straighten out those gals' permanents; and now I'm convinced that we've got what it takes."

"But how did you do it?" Jerry wanted to know.

"Very simply. I just connected switches in parallel with those operating the door-opening mechanism and the rocking chair. I was careful to splice in at a point where you would not notice. My switches are in a clothes closet near the top of the stairs. With them, I was able to take over a couple of your ghosts. For good measure, I stuck my head out of the closet door once and gave that corny laugh. Your imagination did the rest."

"Well, let me tell you," Carl said earnestly, "it gives you a very funny feeling when one of your own ghosts suddenly goes berserk."

"That I can believe," Mr. Arnold said with another chuckle. "If I live to be a hundred, I'll never forget the way you two were staring popeyed at that rocking chair when I tiptoed to the top of the stairs. I've already got my money's worth out of this prank right now, and we still have tomorrow night to go!"   —30—

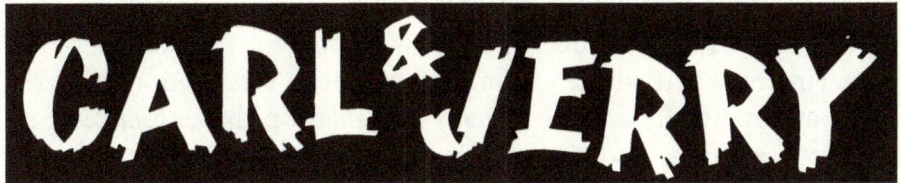

ELECTRONIC TRAP

March 1956

W hat *are* you doing?" Carl demanded lazily, as he turned over on his side on the leather couch to watch his chum, Jerry, who was busily twisting the knobs of a small box sitting on the basement laboratory workbench.

"Deciding whether to take French or Spanish next year," Jerry answered curtly, as he continued to adjust the dials.

Carl heaved his lanky frame erect and strode over to the bench.

"It sounded just as if you said you were deciding whether to take French or Spanish next year," he said laughingly, and peered curiously through his horn-rimmed glasses at the little cabinet studded with knobs, switches and a small meter.

"That's what I *did* say."

"Then you've flipped your wig for sure. I suppose you just say: 'Black box, black box, on the bench, Which shall I take: Spanish or French?' and then this electronic understudy for the Delphic oracle mulls it over for a few microseconds and comes up with the right answer."

"That's not too far off," Jerry said, with a grin on his round face. "This thing is the 'Decision Meter' described back in October 1955 *Popular Electronics*. You can read the article for yourself, but briefly the gadget works like this: When these five dials, which operate potentiometers, are all set at zero, zero voltage appears across this meter. Turning a knob in a counterclockwise direction applies an increasing negative voltage to one terminal of the meter. Turning the knob in the opposite direction applies an increasing positive voltage. I arbitrarily assigned negative values to arguments for French and positive values to arguments in favor of Spanish. As each point came to me, I turned one of the knobs to right or left in accordance with whether Spanish or French was favored by that particular consideration. How far I turned the knob depended upon how important the consideration was. Finally, when all the arguments had been recorded, the instrument automatically and electrically summed up the influence of all the knob settings, and showed by the way the meter was deflected whether Spanish or French was favored. As you can see for yourself, for me personally, Spanish was indicated the better choice."

"Well blow my fuse!" Carl exclaimed. "Imagine us having an electronic brain!"

"That's what it really is, in a modest sort of way. Say, Carl, I want to show you something," Jerry said suddenly, and he went over and opened the cellar door leading to the outside. "See these bad scratches on the outside of the door? Pop is pretty steamed about them. He thinks Bosco is doing it, and he says—and I quote—'Either Carl's got to put boxing gloves on that mutt or give him a close manicure before we have the house repainted this spring'—unquote."

"Bosco wouldn't do a thing like that," Carl denied hotly, getting down on his knees to examine the scratches closely. "In the first place, he's too lazy to scratch that hard."

"Well, I'm neutral, but I have an idea how we can find out what's doing it."

As he finished speaking, Jerry dived into the large junk box beneath the bench and came up with a small dusty chassis bearing two tubes, a couple of knobs, and a relay.

"What's that nasty-looking thing?" Carl asked suspiciously. "I'm not going to have Bosco hurt."

"Don't worry. I'm as fond of that animated flea-garage as you are. This is a capacity relay that will let me know when anything gets close to that door during the night. I built it according to an article that appeared in the very first *Popular Electronics* back in October, 1954."

"How does it work?"

"A sensing wire fastens to this binding post, which is connected to the grid of the triode section of the 12SQ7 tube. This triode section is hooked up as an r.f. oscillator. Some of the r.f. voltage produced by the oscillator is rectified by the diodes of the 12SQ7, and this d.c. voltage is applied as negative grid bias to the 50L6 tube—which has a sensitive relay in its plate circuit. As long as the oscillator is operating strongly, a high bias is produced and the plate current of the 50L6 is low, allowing the relay to stay open. However, if any living thing or large metallic object approaches the sensing wire, the capacity between that object and the wire provides a path through which some of the oscillator energy is drained off. As the oscillation weakens, so does the negative voltage produced by the rectifying diodes. This decreasing negative bias causes the 50L6 plate current through the relay to climb, closing the relay. The closing contacts can turn on a light, ring a bell, or operate any other electrical device."

While talking, Jerry had been installing a short sensing wire along the door jamb and connecting a light bulb so that it could be turned on and off by the relay contacts. After carefully adjusting the sensitivity controls of the capacity relay, he could cause the light bulb to turn on simply by walking within three or four feet of the door. When he stepped back again, the light would go out.

"Now I'll feed this light current through the relay contacts into the pair of wires I have going up to my bedroom," Jerry explained; "and whenever anyone or anything comes close to this door, it will automatically turn on the light up there. That will wake me, without disturbing anyone else, and I can sneak down here and discover Old Scratch —whatever he is—right in the act."

"It sounds just goofy enough to work," was Carl's comment as he started for home. He could not resist waltzing back and forth across the threshold a couple of times to make the light blink on and off before he started climbing the steps that led up to the yard level.

It must have been around two o'clock in the morning when Jerry was awakened by the light that winked on and off a few times in his face and then shone steadily. Quietly, he slipped into his bathrobe and soft-soled slippers, and started for the basement laboratory. When he reached the door that led from the furnace room into the laboratory, he stopped short at the sound coming from the outside laboratory door. It was not a scratching sound. Instead, it sounded more as though some heavy metallic object was being run up and down the edge of the door.

"I always knew old Bosco was plenty smart, but I never thought he knew how to use a crowbar," Jerry marveled to himself.

At that instant there was a sort of crunching sound, and the door swung open. Jerry waited only long enough to see the tall outline of a man step inside and start probing the workbench with the narrow beam of a flashlight held in his hand; then the boy fled silently up the stairs behind him. When he reached the kitchen at the top of the stairs, he debated briefly as to whether or not he should go on upstairs and try to wake up his father; but as he recalled how hard that worthy was to awaken, and how panicky his mother was likely to become, he quickly decided against this. He moved silently into the den and lifted the telephone receiver from the cradle. Silently he gave thanks to his scoutmaster for making every boy in the troop memorize the numbers of the fire department, the police department, and a twenty-four hour ambulance service. Using only his sense of touch, he fumblingly dialed the number of the police department. Although the dial mechanism was really very quiet, its whirring sounded like the grinding of a concrete mixer to the frightened boy— in fact, it made almost as much noise as his pounding heart.

"Police department, Sergeant Anderson speaking," a drawling voice came from the receiver.

"This is Jerry Bishop at 1810 Spear Street. A burglar just broke into our outside basement door on the west side of the house and is prowling around here somewhere right now. Come quick," Jerry whispered hoarsely into the mouthpiece that he was wearing almost like an oxygen mask.

The voice that answered was crisp and businesslike, with all the drawl gone from it: "I gotcha, kid. Don't get in his way. Just lay low. Our squad car will be there in a few seconds. Don't try to answer. He may hear you. Just hang up and make yourself scarce until we get there."

Jerry tried to replace the receiver softly in the cradle, taut at the moment of contact it chattered against the base with a rattle like that of castanets. Holding his breath, Jerry stood there in the dark listening intently. For a few long seconds he heard nothing except the pounding of his heart; then, very softly, there was a familiar creak of the basement stairs. The burglar was coming up to the first floor. Peering through a crack in the door of the den, Jerry could see a suffused glow of light on the kitchen ceiling.

For the next few minutes—which seemed like hours—the boy used his knowledge of the house to keep out of the way of the prowler, who quietly but systematically went about ransacking the whole downstairs. Whenever he found something to his fancy, he chucked it into a burlap sack he carried over his shoulder in true comic-book-burglar fashion. Since he moved very slowly and deliberately, it was not hard for Jerry to keep him in view without being seen himself. At one time the boy thought he heard the sound of a distant car motor, but he could not be sure. He was concentrating so hard on keeping out of the way of that probing flashlight beam that he had scant time to notice anything else.

Suddenly, as the man stood at the bottom of the stairs, a light was turned on in Jerry's room at the head of the stairs. It flickered on and off a couple of times and then went out; but at the first flicker the burglar had switched off his flashlight and moved swiftly toward the kitchen and the stairs leading down into the basement. Jerry, confident that the flickering light from his bedroom had been caused by the police coming through the outside door of the basement, followed warily. Just as he reached the head of the basement stairs, the furnace room below was flooded with light and two policemen with drawn revolvers faced the burglar standing in the middle of the floor.

"Don't move," the tall, lanky policeman commanded. His short, stout partner moved forward and placed a pair of handcuffs on the wrists of the burglar, whose mouth still gaped open with surprise.

"Boy, am I glad to see you guys!" Jerry exclaimed, thumping down the cellar steps. "Those brass buttons on your uniforms look prettier to me right now than any Christmas tree ornament I ever saw!"

"Now there's a heartfelt testimonial," the tall policeman chuckled; "but while the compliments are going around, you've got some coming for keeping cool and using your head. How did you happen to—"

He broke off sharply as strange sounds issued from the adjoining laboratory. There was a scratching at the outside door accompanied by a faint clicking that Jerry recognized as coming from the relay in the capacity-operated unit.

"Sh-h-h! Maybe it's an accomplice," the lanky policeman said, as he moved swiftly across the laboratory to the door and stood poised before it with his revolver tightly clenched in his fist. He jerked the door open and sprang to one side all in a single motion. There in the doorway—with one paw still raised to scratch the disappearing door—stood Bosco, a look of doglike astonishment in his brown eyes. Then he recognized Jerry, and his stubby tail began to vibrate at about sixty cycles per second.

"Come on in, you old rascal," Jerry ordered, and then dropped on his knees and hugged the shaggy dog with almost hysterical affection. "You got caught in the trap, all right, but when Dad hears that because of you we caught a burglar, maybe he won't worry too much about a few little scratches on the cellar door!"   —30—

CARL & JERRY

GOLD IS WHERE YOU FIND IT

April 1956

The bright first-day-of-April sunshine put new life into a fellow; so Carl vaulted nimbly over the low fence that separated his yard from that of his chum, Jerry Bishop. But he stopped short as he caught sight of his friend out on the lawn near the street. On Jerry's head was a pair of huge muff-type airplane earphones that were plugged into a small aluminum box slung from his shoulder. From this box a cord led to the strange device he held in his hands. It consisted of a long broom handle attached to the crosspiece on a large, flat wooden hoop so as to hold this hoop parallel to the ground. Jerry's round face wore a faraway look of abstract concentration as he shuffled along, waving the hoop back and forth over the sprouting grass.

"Hey, Jer, what're you doing?" Carl demanded, when he managed to catch Jerry's vacant eye.

"What did you say?" Jerry asked, sliding the phones forward on his head so that he could hear.

"I asked what you thought you were doing with that contraption."

"You mean my worm-warmer here?" Jerry asked, with bland innocence. "I'm just doing my bit for be-kind-to-worms-week. This is an r.f. induction coil that heats the ground beneath it and makes things comfy for the poor little worms that are still chilled from winter."

"Ask an intelligent question and you get a smart answer," Carl muttered. "Are you going to tell me what that thing is, or am I going to have to squeeze that narrow hoop down over your fat and flabby body?"

"All right; this is a metal locator. I built it from an article by Harvey Pollack that appeared in the June, 1955 issue of *Popular Electronics*."

"How does it work?"

"Inside this aluminum box is an oscillator operating on about two megacycles. Shielded from it is another oscillator whose tank coil, electrostatically shielded, is wound Inside this wooden hoop. Shielded wire connects the outboard tank coil to the rest of its circuit inside the box. The two oscillators are tuned to very nearly the same frequency, so that a low audio difference-frequency beat note is produced by them. This beat note is detected, amplified, and fed to the earphones. When a metallic object appears in the extensive field of the large coil in the hoop, its presence affects this field and so causes a slight frequency shift in the oscillator connected to it. This, in turn, produces an easily detected change in the beat note frequency heard in the phones and warns the operator that the probe coil is nearing some metallic object. Here," Jerry said, as he freed one of the earphones from the- headband; "you walk along behind me and listen, and I'll show you what I mean."

When Carl held the earphone to his ear, he heard a low-pitched musical tone. Suddenly, as Jerry moved the hoop over the grass, the note rose to a high pitch; then it went back down as Jerry kept walking. Probing the area with the coil established that there was a line perpendicular to the curb that gave the same high-pitched sound as the probe was moved along the narrow path; but if the coil were moved to either side of this path, the note in the phones returned to the normal low value.

"What's down there?" Carl asked.

In answer, Jerry followed the invisible object beneath the surface with the metal locator right to the curb, where a large "G" was chiseled in the cement.

"It's the gas line," he explained. "The gas people marked the curb this way when the cement street was laid so that they could find their service lines easily."

"What else is the gadget good for?"

"Locating electric cables and pipes in walls or finding any metallic objects burled In the ground, such as pipes, tanks, or—" Jerry paused dramatically, "—buried treasure!"

Carl's eyes opened wide behind his horn-rimmed glasses. "You're holding out on me!" he accused. "Give!"

Jerry leaned on the handle of the metal locator as he talked: "Saturday, a week ago, old Mr. Gruber and I went up Eel River to the mouth of Tick Creek fishing. They didn't bite very lively, and we did a lot of talking. For once I managed to get him off his favorite subjects of flying saucers and space travel, and he told me an old legend he had heard from his father.

"A flock of years ago, the government bought all this land from an Indian tribe that lived on it. The government paid the Indians $80,000 in gold and gave them a new reservation in the Northwest. An escort of soldiers was to accompany the tribe to its new home.

"While still in the assembly encampment, the Indians heard the soldiers talking and decided, rightly or wrongly, that these soldiers planned to rob them of their gold on the journey; so, secretly, during the dead of night, the elders of the tribe buried the gold on the banks of Eel River. Unfortunately, smallpox broke out among the Indians on their march to their new home, and not a single member of the party that buried the gold survived; consequently, it's still there waiting for someone to find it.

"According to Mr. Gruber, when he was a boy, he and his friends used to hunt for the gold all up and down the river. Later, when he was grown, the legend became a sort of hobby with him, and he read every scrap about it he could find. Out of this study came the conviction that the assembly encampment must have been very near the mouth of Tick Creek and that the gold is buried in that vicinity. Of course, this still leaves a lot of territory to be explored by tedious digging; but with a gadget like this, a person could go over a lot of ground in a hurry—"

"Well, what are we waiting for?" Carl demanded. "I'll get a couple of shovels and a pick, and a tow sack to bring back the loot, and you get your bike. Yo ho ho, and a bottle of rum!"

Tick Creek emptied into Eel River only a short distance above the town; so within the hour the boys had hidden their bicycles in the bushes along the road and were trudging across the cornfield that lay between the road and the thin line of trees marking the river bank.

"Hey, Jer," Carl said, as he strode along-with the digging tools cradled in his arms, "do you think we ought to ask permission from Mr. Sloan, who owns this farm, before we start looking for the gold?"

"Naw," Jerry replied. "In the first place, he's an old crab and would say no automatically. Then, too, I'd feel kind of silly telling him we wanted to go treasure hunting on his farm. He'd think we'd both blown our corks for sure. Of course, if we find anything, we'll tell him and divide up with him."

By the time this serious matter was settled, the boys had reached the point where shallow Tick Creek flowed into Eel River, thrusting a flat sandbar halfway across the larger stream, Jerry at once unlimbered his metal locator and began a systematic survey of the area, while Carl tagged along at his heels breathing down the back of his neck. The boys had been prospecting tor scarcely ten minutes when Jerry suddenly stopped dead in his tracks so abruptly that Carl stumbled into him.

"What is it? What do you hear?" Carl shouted anxiously.

"There's something down there," Jerry said slowly, as he moved the probing hoop around in an exploring circle. "It's right here, and it seems to be about as big around as a small washtub."

As Jerry finished speaking, Carl thrust him aside and began digging feverishly at the spot where the metal locator had given the strongest indication. Even Jerry, who ordinarily had a strong aversion to any kind of physical exercise, grabbed up the other shovel and began turning over the soft earth. The boys quickly sank a shaft about three feet in diameter, and when it had reached such a depth that the edge of the hole came about to Carl's chest, his shovel suddenly gave forth with the hair-raising sound of metal scraping on metal.

"Easy now," Jerry admonished, as he knelt at the side of the hole and peered Intently down to where Carl was gently scraping the dirt away with the edge of the shovel.

"Aw, heck!" Carl suddenly said, with deep disappointment. "It's just a roll of old fence wire."

"And what did you expect?" a gruff voice asked from behind him.

The heads of both boys jerked up to see a scowling farmer, carrying a pitchfork, towering over them.

"What do you young rascals think you're doing?" he demanded. "Now, climb right out of that hole and start filling it up. You think I want one of my cows stepping in that and breaking her leg and making it necessary for me to destroy her? What are you trying to do, anyway?"

As the boys meekly started shoveling the earth back into the hole, they told him about the legend and tried to explain the operation of their metal locator.

"A likely cock-and-bull story!" Mr. Sloan sneered. "I've never held with these scientific gadgets since I gave a fellow with a peach tree fork ten dollars to twitch a well site for me. We drove straight down a hundred and forty feet right where he said and never struck a drop of good water. You just gather up your junk, and I'll personally escort you off my property. And if you know what's good for you, you'll never set foot on it again."

Jerry rigged himself up in his metal locator, and Carl gathered up the tools. All three started across the cornfield toward the road, with Mr. Sloan—his pitchfork cradled in the crook of his arm—following behind Jerry. When they were about halfway across the field, Jerry stopped so abruptly that Mr. Sloan narrowly averted thrusting the tines of the pitchfork into the boy's leg.

"What are you trying to do ... make me hurt you so you can sue me?" Mr. Sloan bellowed. "Keep moving."

"Wait a minute," Jerry said, as he moved the search coil about over the broken cornstalks. "I'm getting an indication of something down here."

He set the probe down, dropped to his knees, and began to scrape away at the soft earth where he had obtained the strong reading. In a

moment he stood up, dangling something from a dirt-encrusted chain that glinted yellowly in the sun.

"Here, let me see that," Mr. Sloan said sharply. He brushed aside more of the clinging dirt and then exclaimed, "Well I'll be danged if it's not my pappy's old watch that I lost when I was checking corn last spring! I sure thought I'd never set eyes on it again, and that grieved me sorely, for I put a great store in that old turnip. The case is heavy gold, and it was given to my father by my mother on their wedding day. See, here's an inscription on the inside. I wouldn't trade it for the finest diamond-studded watch you could buy."

He paused a moment and then went on: "I'm mighty obliged to you boys for finding it for me, and here's five dollars each for you. Take it; I won't have it any other way. What's more, I'm downright ashamed of acting so crabby with you before."

"Aw, that's all right, Mr. Sloan," Jerry said. "We really should have asked your permission before we trespassed on your property anyway. What tickles me, though, is that we were able to prove to you that this gadget, unlike that fellow's peach tree fork, really does what it's supposed to do."

"Well, you certainly convinced me," Mr. Sloan said heartily, with a broad and friendly grin; "and I'll tell you what! I have to take a load of steers to the sales barn today; but if you fellers can come back tomorrow afternoon, I'll get my shovel and go along with you, and we'll comb this old farm of mine with that gold-sniffing gadget of yours to a fare-you-well . . . that is, if you don't mind letting a crabbed old cuss like me in on the fun."

"Tickled to have you, Mr. Sloan!" the boys chorused together. —30—

FEEDBACK

May 1956

You might have thought—if you were a careless observer and didn't know the boys very well—that Carl and Jerry were doing nothing. It must be admitted that they looked idle as they sprawled on the turf of Jerry's back yard under the relaxing rays of the warm May sun. However, you had only to look a little closer to notice the slowly revolving reels on the tape recorder beside them and to see the cord leading from it to a slender microphone mounted in the center of a metal object shaped like a huge shallow dish some three feet in diameter. This was propped up on edge so that its concave side carrying the microphone faced away from the boys toward the hedge separating Jerry's yard from the one next door.

"I think that's a lot of stuff about that king-size popcorn bowl picking up sounds we can't hear," Carl muttered in low tones with a somewhat disparaging glance at it.

"Have it your way," Jerry answered, "but when we play back the tape, you'll hear those birds that are playing around in the hedge now cheeping and twittering as though they were right in front of the microphone. That parabolic reflector focuses the sound waves on the microphone the same way the concave mirrors we play around with in the physics lab at school focus light rays down to a single bright spot. People who collect bird calls and insect sounds use this technique all the time. Just keep your voice down so you don't scare the birds and so the microphone doesn't pick it up."

"Mrs. Selden is the one who should keep her voice down," Carl said, as the shrill complaining of the woman next door came through the hedge.

"They're taking out the storm sash and washing the windows," Jerry reported, after rising to his knees so that he could see over the hedge.

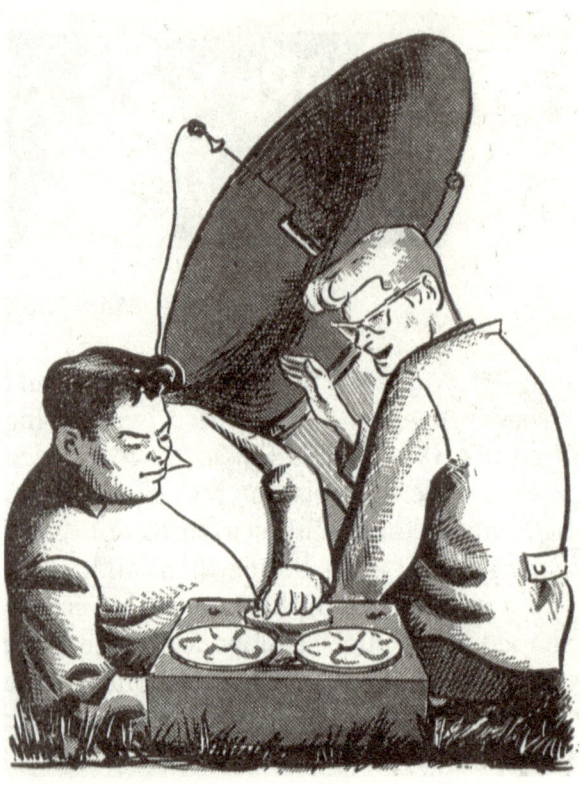

"How come she bends Mr. Selden's ear that way all the time?" Carl asked.

"Habit, I guess. Leastways, that's what Mom thinks. She says Mrs. Selden has been scolding so long she doesn't know she's doing it," Jerry explained with a yawn as he stretched out on the grass again.

"Hey, Jer," Carl said lazily, toying with the rubbery stem of a plucked dandelion, "how's about briefing me a little on negative feedback while we're eavesdropping on the birds? I'm cooking up a new speech amplifier for my ham rig, and I don't know whether to use feedback or not."

"Hokey-dokey," Jerry agreed. "To begin with, feedback is simply the taking of some of the output of a device and feeding it back into the input. As far as an amplifier is concerned, feedback comes in two different flavors: if the portion of the output signal fed back is 'phased' or timed so that it aids or increases the swing of the input signal, it's called 'positive' or 'regenerative' feedback. Positive feedback increases the amplification and results in greater output. But an amplifier with positive feedback has a strong tendency to favor one frequency over the others and so produce harmonic distortion and nonlinear amplification. Worse yet, when enough positive feedback is applied, the circuit breaks into oscillation at essentially this favored frequency, and the circuit then becomes useless as an amplifier. Generally speaking, positive feedback is a darned nuisance in an audio amplifier—it leads to howling, motorboating, and poor performance; but don't forget that when it comes to oscillators, we must have positive feedback or we don't have any oscillation.

" 'Negative,' 'degenerative' or 'inverse' feedback is phased so that the energy returned to the input circuit from the output actually opposes the signal voltage acting on the grid and reduces the amplification. This contrariwise relationship between the plate and grid circuits works to advantage, for any hum or noise or distortion generated in the plate circuit tends to 'buck' itself out. The distorting 'zig' in the plate circuit produces an opposite-going 'zag' in the controlling grid voltage that sends through a correcting signal to help iron out the distortion in the output."

"Hey, that's pretty cute: it's as though the circuit were correcting all its own faults!"

"Yes, negative feedback has several advantages. It reduces output circuit hum, noise, and harmonic distortion by the same percentage that it reduces the gain. When it's applied as it should be, negative feedback evens up the amplification given to different frequencies and makes an amplifier more nearly 'flat' in its frequency response."

"Negative feedback seems to have everything. What's the catch?" Carl wanted to know.

"The only catch Is that it reduces the gain by the same amount that it reduces the distortion. It can only be applied when you have sufficient surplus of gain to sacrifice amplification in order to obtain the other advantages."

"How do you put negative feedback into a circuit?" was Carl's next question.

"An easy way to do it with a single-tube amplifier is to leave the cathode resistor unbypassed. In this case, the cathode resistor becomes a part of the plate load, and a portion of the plate signal voltage appears between the cathode and ground. The voltage across the cathode resistor also appears in series with the signal voltage on the grid, but its polarity opposes that signal voltage. Take a f'rinstance: Say that the signal swings the negatively biased grid less negative. This increases both plate and cathode current. Increased cathode current increases the voltage drop across the cathode resistor, making the cathode more positive with respect to ground. Since the grid is connected to ground, it also makes the cathode more positive with respect to the grid, or the grid more negative with respect to the cathode. This last action opposes the original signal voltage that was driving the grid less negative."

"The amount of feedback in such a, case would be determined by the ratio of the cathode resistor to the plate load resistor, I suppose."

"That's right. An interesting example of 100% negative feedback occurs in the cathode follower circuit in which the plate is grounded, as far as signal voltage is concerned, and the cathode resistor is the entire plate load. In this case, the voltage gain or amplification of the stage is reduced to less than one, but distortion is practically nil."

"I suppose there are other ways of introducing negative feedback."

"Oh, sure. Quite often a lead is run from one side of a speaker voice coil back to the grid or cathode of a preceding stage. By selecting the proper end of the output transformer secondary, you can get a voltage that will constitute 'negative feedback' for any preceding stage. Remember that every time a signal passes through a tube it undergoes a 180° phase shift; so a voltage that would be 'negative feedback' at the grid of one tube would be 'positive feedback' at the grid of a preceding or following stage."

"Then a feedback loop may embrace more than just one tube."

"That's right. It's quite common to feed back for two or three stages."

"I notice you speak about negative feedback being applied to a 'device.' Did you mean to say that?"

"Yes. Feedback is found in a lot more places than audio amplifiers. For example, in a public address system, when the volume is boosted too high, you get positive acoustic feedback from the speaker to the microphone that results in a howl or oscillation. It's interesting to note, incidentally, that this howl usually occurs on a particular note for a given system. Remember we said that positive feedback favored one frequency?

"A fine example of negative feedback applied to a mechanical system," continued Jerry, after taking a deep breath, "is in the governor of a steam engine. This governor consists of two metal balls attached by hinged rods to a vertical shaft that is rotated by the steam engine. As the balls swing toward or away from the shaft, they control a valve that regulates the amount of steam admitted to the engine. When they're resting next to the shaft, the valve is wide open; and the farther they swing out, the more this valve closes. When the engine tries to speed up, the vertical shaft is rotated faster and centrifugal force causes the balls to swing out, cutting down on the steam and slowing down the engine. If the application of a heavy load reduces the speed of the engine, the balls swing in and open the valve, which restores the speed.

"Feedback even plays an important part in our physical actions. For example, notice what happens when I decide to pick up that twig. My brain sends a message to my hand that starts it moving toward the twig. As my hand moves, my eye keeps measuring the distance that still separates my hand from the little branch and constantly reports this information back to the brain. As the distance grows less and less, the information fed back is acted upon to cause my hand to slow down and finally stop directly over the twig."

"In fact," Jerry concluded, as he rolled over to stop the tape recorder and start rewinding the tape, "feedback plays a most important part in electronic brains, guided missiles, and so on. In all these devices, the data, direction, or movement is constantly being sampled and tested and fed back to the controlling mechanism to answer its unceasing need to know 'How am I doing?'"

As he finished speaking, he started the tape playing through the recorder. At first, the only sound was that of the birds chirping away with amazing volume and lifelike clarity. They sounded as though they might have been perched right on the microphone. Suddenly, though, the shrill complaining voice of Mrs. Selden burst through with a "presence" that made both boys jump. She kept up a constant tirade at her husband; he was clumsy; he was going to break the storm sash; he was not washing the windows clean; etc. All he was heard to say in reply was a patient, "Yes, Martha; no, Martha."

Listening to the voices that scarcely could have been more distinct if they had been talking directly into the mike, Carl's face suddenly took on a very thoughtful look. He peeped over the hedge at Mr. and Mrs. Selden, now sitting in their porch swing, and then turned to Jerry.

"Didn't you say applying negative feedback corrected imperfections in the output?" he demanded in a whisper.

"That's right, but so what?"

"Wait here. I'll be right back," Carl ordered, as he left on a stooping run for Jerry's basement laboratory.

He was back very shortly carrying a small extension speaker for the tape recorder. After plugging one end of its long cord into the external speaker jack of the recorder, Carl started crawling with it over to the hedge. Here he set up the speaker so that its cone pointed at the couple in the porch swing only a few feet away. Then he directed Jerry—by means of elaborate motions—to rewind the tape and start it playing again. Jerry carried out the pantomimed instructions and then crawled over to his chum.

"Those birds in the hedge certainly are happy today," Mr. Selden remarked, when the first part of the tape started playing. In a few minutes, Mrs. Selden's voice issued through the speaker.

"Where can that woman with such a mean voice be?" Mrs. Selden wanted to know, as she listened to the constant scolding. "If I were her husband I'd tell her off—why, Jim, that sounds like your voice!"

As she continued to listen, a slow flush crept over the face of Mrs. Selden. In the beginning, she had not recognized her own voice; but the familiar words and phrases soon left no doubt in her mind as to who the speaker was. She turned to her husband— whose face was wearing a look that was apprehensive, embarrassed, and reassuring all at once—and looking at him with eyes brimming with tears, she said gently, "Jim, I never realized I sounded like that. I don't see how you put up with me."

"Don't say that, Martha," he replied gently, as he placed an arm about her quaking shoulders. "I don't really mind at all. I know you don't mean it. It's just your way of talking."

"It *was* my way of talking," she corrected, snuggling against his shoulder. "As long as I live, I will never, never talk to you like that again."

As she finished speaking, she lifted a tear-stained face to her husband's, and the boys beat a hasty, wriggling retreat to Jerry's basement, carrying the extension speaker with them.

"Say," Carl demanded, "are you sure that was *negative* feedback we were using on Mrs. Selden?"

"It must have been," Jerry said, with a, broad grin. "You heard for yourself that it was going to improve her performance. Why do you ask?"

"Well, it looked to me as if they were about to break into osculation when we left, and I thought you said only *positive* feedback caused —"

He was not able to finish because Jerry, who hated puns, flipped a loop of the extension speaker cord over his chum's neck and pulled the ends taut.   —30—

GENIUSES AT WORK

For an hour, Carl and Jerry had been working away on separate projects at opposite ends of the workbench in their basement laboratory. Each was too stubborn to ask what the other was doing, but the puzzled glances each of them sneaked at the other's equipment from time to time revealed how great was the strain. Finally Jerry cracked.

"So, okay; I give up. What are you doing with that timer clock, making a time bomb?"

"Not at all," Carl answered, taking off his horn-rimmed glasses and wiping them with a very dubious-looking handkerchief. "You know what a large charge I get out of these bright, warm, sunny, sparkling summer mornings. I don't want to miss a single one of them, and this timer clock I built from that article in the May 1955 issue of *Popular Electronics* will make sure that I won't. A 110-volt a. c. electric gong that used to be in a fire station is plugged into the 'turn on' outlet on the back of the timer and converts it into an electric alarm clock that nobody, but *nobody,* can ignore."

"At the same time," Carl continued, "you know that my second love is sleeping, and nothing gripes me quite so much as to have that gong bounce me out of bed only to discover it's a cloudy or rainy morning good only for staying in the sack. What I'm doing now is taking out insurance against such a revolting development. This sun-battery photocell will be mounted outside my window where the rays of the rising sun can shine directly on it. Leads will go from the cell to a sensitive relay whose contacts close only when direct sunlight falls on the cell. These contacts are inserted in one of the leads going to the gong, and—"

"I get it," Jerry broke in, admiringly. "If it's a cloudy day, the relay contacts will stay open and keep the timer from ringing the gong; but if the sun is shining, then the timer clock will wake you—and doubtless the rest of the household—at the time for which it is set. My boy, you're a real brain!"

"Really nothing," Carl said, with airy modesty. "What are you doing there?" "Well," Jerry said hesitantly, "I guess you might say I was making a mug-trap." "You're not getting through to me. Try another wavelength."

"It's this way," Jerry explained. "My Uncle Walter, who lives on a farm just south of town, has something very funny going on in his henhouse. About every other night, something or somebody —probably the latter—goes into the henhouse, tears up the hens' nests, and scatters them all over the floor."

"Why do you say it's probably 'somebody'?"

"Because my uncle thinks that only a human being would be able to unfasten the rather complicated latch on the door. He says, too, that if it were a fox or a skunk or a weasel, such an animal would kill the chickens and eat them; but all the mysterious visitor does is scare heck out of the hens. They're so nervous that their egg-laying is falling off."

"A hen with a nervous breakdown is something I've got to see," Carl said with a grin, "but where do you fit into all this?"

"Uncle Walt, who realizes I'm an electronic genius, wants me to help him catch the critter, or at least to find out what it is. He doesn't want to use any ordinary kind of trap because he suspects that maybe kids are doing the mischief, and naturally he wouldn't want to hurt them. At the same time, he doesn't want just to sit around and have his prize hens scared silly."

"What've you got in mind?"

"I can show you a lot easier than tell you. Why don't you go out to Uncle Walt's with me and stay all night? You can tell your mom I invited you."

"It's a deal! Wait until I get my leg-power hot rod, and I'll be right with you. I've got to see this *Strange Case of the Harassed Hens* to a finish."

Carl's mother had no objection, and soon the boys were riding their bikes toward the farm. As was always the case when something interesting was in prospect, they didn't use the seats of the bicycles much, and they soon arrived at the prosperous-looking farm of Jerry's uncle. Uncle Walt was a tall lean man with bright blue eyes set deep in a lined and weathered face. After Jerry had introduced Carl and explained that he was going to stay all night, the man turned to his nephew and said, "Well, how about it, Marconi? Are you all set to give our mysterious visitor his comeuppance?"

"I think so, Uncle Walt. If you don't mind. Carl and I will get busy right away setting up the—the—the device."

"Be my guests, boys!" Uncle Walt said with a grin, waving toward the neat, well-painted chicken house. "I'll go and start the milking."

"First," Jerry said, as he started unloading the cardboard box he had brought along, "we'll mount this normally closed Microswitch on the door jamb so that its contacts are held open by the closed door, and so that the contacts will close just as soon as the door starts to open. As you can see, the switch is inserted in one wire of this line cord, which will go from an outlet socket inside the chicken stable to the rotary solenoid fastened to this board with the camera."

"Hold it! What exactly is a rotary solenoid?"

"It's a solenoid that twists a shaft through an arc of several degrees when current is applied to it, instead of moving a plunger like an ordinary solenoid does. The little arm fastened to the rotating shaft connects through this small spring to the shutter release of the camera. And notice that at the end of the little arm's travel it flips this toggle switch from *on* to *off*."

"Two questions: why use the spring, and what does the toggle switch do?"

"The first thought of any experimenter or technician worth his salt is to protect his equipment against possible damage, and that's the function of both the spring and the switch. This rotary solenoid is very fast-acting, and I was afraid it might injure the camera unless a shock-absorbing linkage

was used between the arm and the shutter release. Also, this solenoid is intended only for intermittent use and would overheat and be destroyed if current were allowed to remain on it for a long period of time, as would happen if the door of the chicken house were left ajar. The switch is in series with the Microswitch and takes the voltage off the solenoid after it has done its job of tripping the camera. What's more, with this switch in the *off* position, the door can be opened without tripping the camera—an important factor in setting things up, testing, or using the door during daylight hours when we don't need to have the trap set."

"Where will the camera be placed?"

"Back inside this box to protect it from the weather. The lens will be focused on the door, and when the solenoid trips the shutter, the synchronized flash will light up the whole area, providing us with a fine 'mug-shot' of whoever or whatever is fooling with the door."

Carl walked slowly around, studying the layout from all angles.

"I see only one thing wrong," he finally remarked. "If the prowler is human, the firing of the flash bulb is bound to show him where the camera is. What's to prevent his taking camera, evidence, and all along with him?"

"That's using the old hat-rack!" Jerry applauded. "Since it's my camera, that worried me, too. But I've got the solution right here." As he said this, he reached down into the cardboard carton and pulled out an electric bell. "This bell will be connected across the line cord going to the solenoid. It'll be behind the Microswitch but ahead of the toggle switch. That way it'll start to ring as soon as the door is opened, and will keep on ringing until the door is closed or until we come out and shut it off. Beast or human, it would have to be an iron-nerved character to stick around with this bell clanging away."

With the plan clearly in mind, the boys set to work and completed the installation in short order. They put the box housing the camera at one side of the door where it would be most likely to get a good profile shot of anyone looking down at the latch. When everything was in place, Jerry flipped the toggle switch on the camera mounting board to *off* and plugged the line cord into a receptacle inside the building. Instantly the electric bell began to ring loudly; but it stopped when the door was closed. Jerry thrust a bulb into the flashgun mounted on the camera and called to his uncle who was just going to the house with a brimming bucket of milk dangling from each arm:

"Uncle Walt, will you want to go into the chicken house any more during the evening?"

"Nope, I'm all through in there; so you can set your trap. Then you boys come on up to the house and wash up for supper. It ought to be about ready."

After one more final inspection of the wiring, Jerry flipped the toggle switch to *on* and the boys followed Mr. Bishop to the house. There, Mrs. Bishop, who looked a lot more like a club woman than a "typical" farm wife, served a fine country meal consisting of golden-brown store-dressed fried chicken, ready-mixed light biscuits covered with plenty of good yellow margarine, and a dessert of commercially quick-frozen strawberries spread over large mounds of luscious vanilla ice cream from the local ice cream plant.

This huge meal and the outdoor exercise the boys had had made them so sleepy that they were barely able to stay awake until nine o'clock. Right after that, they all went to bed.

It seemed to Jerry that his head had barely touched the pillow before he found himself sitting bolt-upright in bed, staring into the darkness, while the distant ringing of a bell came through the open window. Nimbly he hopped out on the floor and switched on the light, only to discover that Carl was already tugging his pants on over his pajamas.

"Sounds like we got a rat in our trap," Carl grunted, as he tried to wriggle a bare foot into his shoe.

The boys pounded down the stairs and out into the barnyard. The bobbing circle of light from Mr. Bishop's flashlight guided them to the hen house where Uncle Walt, a double-barreled shotgun cradled in the crook of his arm, stood looking at the open door of the building.

"Whatever the thing was, it took off when the bell started to ring," he told the wide-eyed youths, "but if your contraption worked, you should have his calling card inside the camera."

An examination with the aid of the flashlight revealed that the toggle switch had been flipped to *off*, indicating that the camera shutter had been tripped. Jerry removed the camera from the board and advanced the film to the next exposure.

"It's only two AM, so we may as well go back to bed," Uncle Walter suggested, as he closed and latched the door. "I'll see you young buckeroos at breakfast."

For a few minutes after getting back in bed, Carl and Jerry were too excited to go to sleep. But they soon calmed down and drifted off into slumber. They knew nothing more until Jerry's Aunt Enid knocked at their door and told them that breakfast was ready.

The boys bolted their breakfast pancakes and sausage in short order. They paused only long enough to take a couple of pictures of Mr. and Mrs. Bishop, "just to finish off the roll," as they unflatteringly put it before they hopped on their bicycles and headed back for town and the darkroom Carl had fixed up in a corner of his basement.

Inside this room, with the red safelight turned on, Jerry removed the roll of Verichrome film from the camera, stripped off the backing paper, and attached clips to the ends while Carl filled one tray with developing solution, another with clear water, and a third with hypo. A quick check with a thermometer showed that by one of those happy coincidences that *do* happen occasionally, the solutions were exactly at 68 degrees. Carl passed the strip of film through the clear water a couple of times and then began to seesaw it gently and methodically through the tray of developing solution. After a couple of minutes, Jerry, whose head had been bobbing up and down with the movement of the film as he tried to make out the emerging negative pictures, muttered:

"We didn't draw a blank, anyway; there's something on every frame."

After a couple more minutes of passing the film through the developer, Carl transferred it to the clear water for a few passes and then began to seesaw it through the tray of hypo. When he had done this for several minutes, he stopped and turned on the white light.

"By golly, it's a midget burglar!" Jerry declared, looking over at the negative which was third from one end of the strip of film Carl had developed.

"Burglar, my eye!" Carl said with a grin. "That's a raccoon, and a big fat one at that. All raccoons have that distinctive mask-marking around the eyes. There's something around his neck I can't make out on the negative. Let me finish fixing, washing, and drying the film. Then we'll make a print so that we can really see the details."

An hour both boys were examining a fine large print of the raccoon, which must have been staring directly at the camera when the flash bulb went off. It was standing on its hind legs, and its little paws still had hold of the latch. Around its neck was a leather collar with a metal plate fastened to it.

"That must be a pet raccoon," Jerry said. "I'll run upstairs and tell Uncle Walter, and see what he knows about it."

In a few minutes, he came back into the darkroom with a broad grin on his face.

"The mystery is solved. Uncle Walt says that the raccoon is a pet of a boy who lives on the next farm. It's so tame that they just let it run loose like a dog. It must have been prowling around Uncle Walt's farm when it discovered how to open the chicken house door—raccoons are very clever about things like that—and then had itself a real ball scaring the hens. This was so much fun, evidently, that the raccoon came back and did it again every night or so. Uncle Walt called the boy, and he promised to keep Mr. Raccoon tied up at night.

"Another victory for the electronic raccoon hunters!" Carl remarked," starting to put away the developing materials.   —30—

ANCHORS AWEIGH

July 1956

It was a beautiful July day. The warm sun sparkled on the little ripples produced by the gentle breeze moving over the broad expanse of backwater above the dam in the St. Joseph River, and there were just enough white clouds drifting in the sky to bring out its deep summer blue.

All this natural beauty was wasted on Carl and Jerry, however. As they knelt on the bank, their admiration was entirely focused on the gleaming brasswork of the three-foot-long radio-controlled model tugboat resting on the ground between them.

"I still say it was a dirty gyp not to let me help put it together," Carl complained.

"But I *told* you my uncle in the Navy sent me the plans for the boat, plus the motor and the radio-control equipment from England," Jerry said patiently. "He wrote that he wasn't going to have an ignorant land-lubber swab for a nephew if he could help it, and that I was to build the thing *all by myself* and have it ready for his inspection when he arrives next month on leave. If I had let you help me put it together—and I really ached to show it to you—that would have been cheating."

"Well, all right," Carl said grudgingly, "but let's get started. I want to see it work."

"First," Jerry began, as he took out three bottles from a box beside him, "we've got to mix the fuel. This water-cooled diesel motor runs on equal parts of ether, castor oil, and kerosene."

"If you don't mind, I'll move upwind while you mix," Carl said, hastily scrambling to his feet. "I've got a grandmother who thinks castor oil is good for whatever ails boys, and Mom believes everything Grandma says. As a result, I know I've taken enough castor oil to float

165

that boat easily; and I just can't stand the smell of the stuff. How much moxie does that motor have?"

"It has five cubic centimeters piston displacement, and will develop a full ½ B.H.P. at 12,000 rpm."

"A half horsepower, huh? That's a real powerhouse! But then, I suppose a tug should have power. How about the radio controls?"

"I built up a sensitive three-tube receiver to go with the six-channel reed bank my uncle sent over. Servos operating with the reed selector unit give me any degree of right or left rudder, and I have full control of the motor speed from idle to full-throttle. Since the diesel won't run backward, I can't reverse the boat yet; but I hope to have a gear-box installed in there pretty soon that will let me reverse it. The unused channels will be used at a later date to carry out some big plans I have."

The boys put the fuel into the motor fuel tank and checked out the radio controls. Jerry plugged a milliammeter into a jack on the boat receiver and tuned the input circuit to the frequency of the transmitter, with the meter serving as tuning indicator. Then they watched the operation of the servos connected to the rudder and throttle arm as the buttons on the remote control transmitter case were depressed. Everything worked perfectly, and they were just preparing to start the motor when a harsh, high-pitched voice behind them demanded:

"What're you kids fixing to do?"

They turned around to see a sour-visaged old man standing beside a boat tied to the bank. Under his arm were several long cane poles, and he carried a battered minnow bucket in each hand.

"We're just going to try out our radio-controlled boat," Jerry explained politely.

"I knew it!" the man exclaimed with triumphant satisfaction. "I just felt in my bones you were up to some devilment like that. Well, let me tell you brats something: I'm going out there in the middle of the river to fish for crappie, and when I fish I want things quiet. That silly contraption had better not come within a hundred yards of my boat, or you'll be sorry. Do you get that?"

"We'll keep the model away from your boat," Jerry promised.

Muttering to himself, the old man loaded his paraphernalia into his boat and shoved off. As he leisurely rowed toward the middle of the wide river, the boys exchanged glances.

"Gee, what a grouch!" Carl exclaimed. "I had a big notion to tell him off."

"I'm glad you didn't," Jerry said slowly. "In the first place, he's an old man and should be shown respect. More important, though, is the fact that his hobby of fishing is just as important to him as our hobby of playing with this boat is to us. He's probably been fishing here for a long, long time and has a right to keep on doing so without interruption.

"Anyway, I'd just as soon not send the tugboat out any distance today. We'll keep it here close to the bank while we become familiar with the controls. Then, too, I want to see which one of these propellers I brought along will provide the most push. Running the motor for only short stretches at a time should help to break it in."

Without further talk, the boys started the motor and gently placed the little boat in the water. It rode beautifully as they sent it in tight circles close to the bank, and they were deeply gratified at how quickly and completely it responded to signals sent out by the transmitter. Then Jerry fastened a line from one of the towing irons at the stern of the little tug, and fastened the other end of the line to a spring scale held just above the surface of the water. Carl pushed the full-throttle button on the transmitter, and the popping exhaust suddenly rose to a high-pitched whine. The water boiled up behind the stern of the little vessel as it squatted low in the water to pull with all its might against the scale.

They noted the measured pull of the boat and then placed another propeller on the drive shaft and repeated the test. One propeller of the four eventually tried showed several ounces more pull than any of the rest; so the boys left it on the shaft. Then they refilled the fuel tank and prepared to proceed with their next experiment: trying to "dock" an old railroad tie floating leisurely past by pushing against it with the fender around the tug's bow.

"Old Sourpuss must have caught one," Carl commented, as he rose from placing the boat back in the water, and glanced out to where

the old man was standing up in his boat a couple of hundred yards away.

"No; he's pulled in the anchor and is letting the boat drift with the breeze. I've been watching him. He ought not be standing up in a narrow boat that way, though—"

Jerry broke off with a gasp as the old man, who had been transferring a minnow bucket from one side of the boat to the other, suddenly lost his balance and toppled out of the boat backward, the minnow bucket still clutched in his hands. The departing thrust of his feet gave the boat a shove and it was a good thirty feet away when his head bobbed to the surface.

"Help! Help" the choked voice of the old man came faintly to the boys.

"Can't you swim?" Carl called through the megaphone his cupped hands made.

"Nary a stroke," was the answer. "This minnow bucket is holding me up, but it leaks and won't last long."

Carl sat down on the grass and began tearing at his shoelaces.

"That's too far to swim," Jerry said desperately. "He'll have gone under long before you get there."

"I've gotta try. We can't just sit here and watch him drown."

"The tugboat! The tugboat!" Jerry exclaimed, as his eyes lighted on the puttering little model that slowly had put out from shore while it was left unattended. He pushed a button on the transmitter case, and the motor exhaust rose to a scream of power as the tug shot ahead. It performed a graceful arc and hurtled across the surface of the water.

"What are you going to do?" Carl demanded, watching the swiftly narrowing gap between the little tug and the head of the old man—which could just be seen in the water beyond the drifting rowboat. "That little model will never keep him afloat. It might if he were careful, but he's too excited to think. He'll capsize the tug at his first grab."

"Don't forget that this is a tugboat we've got," Jerry remarked, without taking his eyes off the little radio-controlled craft. As he spoke, the little boat's motor slowed to an idle, and it settled down in the water as it moved slowly ahead to nuzzle its prow against the square stern of the rowboat. Then Jerry pushed a button and the motor again revved up to full-throttle. The rowboat lazily moved ahead toward the head of the old man. Just as it was almost within reach of his outstretched hand, it turned aside; Jerry had pushed the wrong button and the bow of the little model slipped off the transom of the rowboat.

"Hey, what are you doing?" Carl demanded accusingly.

"This is tricky," Jerry explained desperately. "Ya gotta make the tugboat go to the right when you want the rowboat to go to the left."

As he talked, he sent the little boat in a tight circle and brought it into position once more. This time he successfully maneuvered the rowboat into the reach of the barely floating man.

As soon as the old man had safely hold of something substantial, the paralyzing fear went out of him. He moved hand over hand along the side of the boat to the square stern and then pulled himself into the boat over the transom. After resting a few seconds, he took in his poles and started rowing toward the boys, keeping an interested watch on the little tug that performed triumphant circles around him as he rowed along.

"Well, boys, I just don't know what to say," he admitted candidly, stepping out on the shore. "I know as sure as I'm standing here that if weren't for you two and that dandy little boat of yours I'd be dead right now. But I can't seem to think of any way to tell you how much I thank you."

"Don't worry about that," Jerry said, with a friendly grin. "We're just tickled to pieces that everything worked so well."

"This much I *have* to say," the old man went on. "I sure feel bad about the way I talked to you two a little while ago. From now on in, as far as I'm concerned, you can run that wonderful little contraption right up and down my backbone any time you please."

"Then maybe you'd like to come down here tomorrow and watch us try it out for some speed runs," Carl suggested.

"I'd be proud to," the old man said promptly. "Fact is, I'm kind of hankering to have one of those things myself. While I was rowing in, I had the idea that if a man trolled a pork-rind spinner off the back of that thing there's no telling how many bass he might take! And he could just sit here on the bank and smoke his pipe while he was doing it, too!" —30—

BOSCO HAS HIS DAY

August 1956

It was evening, and the boys were sitting on the back steps of Jerry's house. Carl had Bosco, his dog, firmly clamped between his knees and was wooling the dog's ears affectionately while Bosco growled in mock protest at this treatment that he actually loved.

"You stupid, no-account, dumb mutt," Carl muttered softly, as he looked morosely out at the long shadows creeping across the back lawn.

"What's Bosco done now?" Jerry wanted to know.

"It's what he hasn't done—or won't do," Carl replied. "A couple of days ago, as I was riding home on my bike after swimming, I ran across a fellow about our age working with a bird dog in a field out at the edge of town. He would hide a little cloth-covered ball that he called a 'bird' and send the dog in search of it. In nothing flat that dog would sniff out the bird and come trotting back to the guy with it in his mouth. This was interesting, and I was enjoying talking with the joker, but all at once he sort of looked down his nose at Bosco and wanted to know what kind of a dog *that* was.

"I said Bosco was just a plain dog, which seemed to strike him as really hilarious. Anyway, he gave out with a nasty laugh, and started a lot of who-shot-John about how he had papers for *his* dog, called Golden Arrow III, and that unless a dog had breeding you couldn't expect him to amount to much.

"Well, I got my back up at this, and remarked that it took more than a few sheets of paper to make a dog smart. I should have stopped there, but I got carried away and went on to say that if I couldn't teach Bosco to do everything Golden Arrow III was doing within a couple of weeks I'd eat my beanie. This character, whose name is Merrill, promptly took me up on it and said that if Bosco could equal Golden Arrow's performance *he* would eat *his* beanie."

171

"Well, how's it look?"

"Let me put it this way: Do you think white or red sauce would go best with my beanie? I still believe old Bosco here is as smart as any dog that ever chased a cat, but I learn to my sorrow that he has a serious physical defect: He can't smell."

"Can't smell? I thought all dogs had a keen scent."

"So did I, but you can take my word for it that Bosco couldn't follow the trail of a ten-pound limburger cheese dragged over the ground 30 seconds before. By actual scientific tests, I have found that the absolute limit of his sense of smell is sniffing out a dog biscuit at a distance of two feet. Beyond that—nothing! I don't mind losing the bet so much, but I do hate to have poor Bosco made to look like a dummy simply because he can't smell so hot."

"Maybe you could teach him to locate the bird by sight."

"Not a chance. I have to hide the bird for Golden Arrow, and Merrill will hide it for Bosco. I know from watching-him that he'll hide the bird down under leaves and stuff so it can't be seen. And, anyway, I can't make Bosco *want to* find that little cloth-covered ball. He's too smart to work for nothing and displays about as much interest in locating that artificial bird as I show in helping Mom find the castor oil bottle when I'm not feeling well."

"Let's not give up too easy," Jerry said, as his interest in the problem began to mount. "Maybe we can appeal to one of Bosco's baser instincts. What does he like?"

"That's easy. Bosco's interested in just one thing, twenty-four hours a day: *food.* He's a real glutton."

"Then we'll start with that. I'm getting an idea. Remember that description of the transistorized golf ball in *Popular Eectronics* some months back? You'll recall that the golf ball had a tiny transistor transmitter built right into it that sent out a continuous signal. This signal was picked up on a transistor-type receiver and led the owner of the ball right to it, no matter how well it was hidden."

"What's that got to do with making a bird dog out of Bosco?"

"Suppose we build a tiny transmitter into the artificial 'bird' you hide from Bosco. Then we'll fit him with a hidden receiver that will pick up the signal from the transmitter. In a short time, he should learn that when the signal gets stronger *he* must be getting closer—that is, he should be able to learn it if he's as smart is you say he is."

"Oh, he can learn that all right if he wants to, but what's going to make him want to?"

"We'll 'condition' him to expect food as a reward for finding the bird and bringing it to you," Jerry explained. "After he gets used to wearing the receiver, which we'll conceal in some sort of headgear, we turn on the receiver and let him hear the sound of the hidden bird. Then we drag him to the bird, put it into his mouth, clamp his mouth shut, and drag him back to where you're standing. The instant you take the bird out of his mouth, you replace it with a dog biscuit. After we do this a few dozen times, he should get the idea and go find the bird by himself."

"So let's get going!" Carl exclaimed, as he slapped his hands on his knees and rose to his feet. "I'm willing to try anything, even an idea as crazy as that."

With the enthusiasm of youth that enables it to undertake blithely something an older and wiser person—fully appreciating the difficulties—would never start, the two boys dashed down into Jerry's basement laboratory and immediately started building up the electronic equipment designed to convert Bosco from a biscuit dog to a bird dog.

Carl built the small one-transistor transmitter according to a plan for an i.f. signal alignment generator. This tiny little unit delivered an r.f. signal, tone-modulated, on a frequency that could be adjusted from about 400 to 500 kilocycles. Two extra-small penlite batteries furnished the power, and the whole thing fit neatly into a safety match box that in turn was mounted inside a cloth-covered little plastic box selected to serve as the body of the artificial bird.

Jerry had the harder job of building a fixed-tuned receiver for picking up the weak signal from the tiny transmitter. In order to keep size to a minimum, he used a circuit employing two transistors and a crystal diode in a regenerative circuit. Careful planning and layout, dispensing with sockets and soldering leads directly, employing the smallest of miniature parts—and similar space-conserving measures—produced a receiver on a very tiny flat fiberboard chassis. This chassis was sewn into the crown of a boldly checked "Sherlock Holmes" type of hat the boys cajoled Carl's mother into making for them. Bosco was then made to wear this hat in a rather unconventional manner. The normal fore-and-aft projections were pulled down tightly over his ears and fastened under his chin, and a dynamic earphone was concealed in one of the flaps so that it would be held close to the dog's ear.

Do not think that all this was done overnight and that everything worked perfectly as soon as it was put together. Designing electronic equipment just doesn't work that way, not even in commercial laboratories where the finest engineers work with the best equipment. There is always a period of de-bugging, adjusting, and peaking. It took the boys a full three days to build up the two pieces of equipment, to squeeze the last microwatt of power out of the little transmitter, and to peak up the receiver for maximum stable sensitivity. Finally, though, the receiver was capable of picking up the transmitter over the restricted radius that Carl said would be more than adequate for the test that was planned.

Then the equipment was introduced to Bosco, and it certainly was not a case of love at first sight. He spent the first half hour after the cap was fastened on him in a determined effort to shake it off, rub it off on the ground or the trunks of trees, and—finally—to claw it off with all four paws. But the boys had anticipated this, and the cap stayed firmly in place. Finally Bosco gave up and stared at his masters with a hurt look that said plainly, "How can you guys do this to me?"

The boys promptly started his training along the lines Jerry had outlined. It was quickly apparent that Jerry's estimate of "a few dozen" times being needed to show Bosco what was expected of him was highly optimistic. By the time he began to show some faint interest whenever the hidden switch in his cap turned on the receiver and let him hear the signal from the concealed transmitter, the sod of Jerry's backyard was deeply furrowed with hundreds of tracks made by Bosco's stubbornly braced legs as he was dragged back and forth, and both boys were worn to a frazzle. But they stuck at it. Finally, on the last evening before the test, things looked pretty good; and as Jerry wearily took leave of his friend, he said: "That's about all we can do. Don't feed Bosco tomorrow morning, for we really want him eager."

"Okay, but Bosco the Bottomless Pit would be eager anyway. I'll see you tomorrow."

When the boys and Bosco arrived at the little field in which the test was to take place, Merrill, Golden Arrow, and a gentleman with a stopwatch prominently displayed in his hand were already there. "Boys, I thought we should have an impartial judge for this test; so I brought along my Uncle Milford. He's known all over the country for his work with bird dogs," Merrill explained.

"Thank you, Nephew," Uncle Milford said, with a fond smile. "Now I suppose we may as well get on with this. To be fair, I think the winner should be the dog that finds his bird quickest in three times out of five trials. You can hide the bird for Golden Arrow, boy, and Merrill can hide it for—for—what on earth is that on your animal's head?" he exclaimed to Carl as he took a good look at Bosco jauntily wearing his ludicrous cap.

"Bosco is a dog of many parts," Carl explained glibly, "and he likes to dress for each role he plays. Since he feels he's playing a sort of detective right now, he insisted on wearing his Sherlock Holmes cap this morning."

Uncle Milford looked strangely at Carl as he muttered, "I see," in tones that clearly indicated he didn't. "Well, you hide Arrow's bird and we'll start."

Carl tucked the artificial bird Merrill handed him beneath a bush some 75 feet away, and then Merrill sent Golden Arrow in search of it with a wave of his hand. Instantly the dog started quartering the ground in a methodical manner that was beautiful to watch, and in a short time his body stiffened as he caught the scent of the hidden bird; then at a command from Merrill he moved forward, picked it up in his mouth, and returned it to his master.

"Forty-seven seconds!" Uncle Milford announced triumphantly. "Now let's see what the other dog can do."

Merrill tucked Bosco's bird under a clump of leaves about the same distance away that Golden Arrow's had been. When Uncle Milford gave the signal, Carl nipped the hidden switch in Bosco's cap with results that were truly galvanic. Bosco gave a whimper of eagerness as he stood straight up on his hind legs and waltzed crazily about.

Then he dropped to all fours and went dashing madly about the place without apparent rhyme or reason, but in an amazingly short time he rooted down through the leaves to the hidden bird and came galloping back to Carl with slobbers of anticipation dripping from his mouth.

"Fourteen seconds!" Uncle Milford said, in an awed voice. "It doesn't seem possible. I've never seen anything like it. It must have been an accident."

But it was no accident, as the next two trials quickly proved. Golden Arrow III, displaying the same beautifully consistent method and form, turned in times very close to forty-five seconds on both occasions; but Bosco, using his own crazy system that sent him dashing full-tilt, only to come to such an abrupt halt that he often went rolling end-over-end before he scrambled up and took off on a tangent, located his second bird in twenty-two seconds and his third in the astounding time of six seconds flat.

"Well, Merrill, I guess there's no question about the winner," Uncle Milford said, with a stunned look. "I've lever seen anything like the way that dog performs. Very unorthodox! Very! Would you consider entering him in some field trials, boy?"

"Aw, no," Carl said casually, as he unfastened the cap from Bosco's head and let the dog give himself an ear-slapping shake. "Bosco doesn't mind putting on a little show like this now and then, just for relaxation, but he's got much more serious things on his mind than fiddling round with anything so silly as hunting artificial birds."

There was a long pause, and then Uncle Milford inquired timidly:

"May I ask what sort of things?"

Carl looked cautiously around before he answered in hushed tones: "All I'm allowed to tell you is that it's top-secret research in the commissary department. And speaking of eating, Merrill, as soon as you've decided how you're going to prepare your beanie, let Jerry and me know and we'll be glad to drop over to watch you eat it."

"All right, fellows," Merrill said weakly. I'll let you know."   —30—

ELECTRONIC BEACH BUGGY

September 1956

It was a blistering hot last-of-August day, and Carl and Jerry were at the beach, but they were not swimming. Instead, they lolled in the scanty shade of spindly growth on the side of a sand dune and looked disconsolately across the absolutely empty beach at the close-spaced row of large signs sticking in the sand along the edge of the water. The signs read: "DANGER! Water Polluted with Acid. Stay Out!"

A Great Lakes tanker loaded with acid had been in a collision just off shore and lost most of its cargo. This highly concentrated acid, blown in to shore by the wind, had collected on the sand and rocks of the beach. While it was slowly diluting, there was still enough left to cause serious burns to the skin and even more damage to the eyes if it came in contact with them.

"A fine kettle of fish this is," Carl growled. "Here is as hot a day as we've had all summer; there is all of Lake Michigan ready to cool us off; and for all the good it's doing us, we might as well be out in the middle of the Sahara Desert."

"While you're wallowing in self-pity, don't forget that school is coming up like thunder," Jerry added. "In about a week the beach will be OK again, but we'll be sweating it out in the brain factory."

Both boys contemplated this gloomy prospect in silence for a little while, and then Carl said: "Jer, have you dreamed up any ideas yet about how we can raise some money to buy the transistors, special transformers, tiny capacitors, and other parts we'll need for our transistor experiments this winter?"

"Nope, I've not come up with a thing. How about you?"

"Me, neither," Carl replied as he looked across the empty beach, "unless—"

"Unless what?" Jerry demanded, raising himself on an elbow to follow Carl's glance.

"Unless we could do a little beachcombing. You know how packed this place normally is, especially on weekends. There's hardly room to set down a bottle of suntan lotion. Think of all the coins that must have slipped from upside-down pockets into the sand, of all the rings and watches that have been removed to take a plunge and lost, of all the cigarette lighters, bracelets—"

"Okay, okay!" Jerry interrupted. "So what do we do? Sift the sand?"

"A good electronics man like you ought to be ashamed to think of anything so crude and mechanical as that," Carl chided. "We can use our handy-dandy metal locator that we built from the article in the June 1955 *Popular Electronics*. You know how we found Farmer Sloan's gold watch out in the cornfield with it; well, most of the valuables here will only be covered with an inch or so of sand, and the metal locator should be able to sniff them out easily. Only one thing's wrong: that treasure-finder is a little heavy to use over a long period of time, and I just know who will be elected to carry it. Lugging that thing around out there in the hot sun does not appeal—"

"Hold it! I've got an idea," Jerry broke in. "Suppose we mount that little gasoline washing machine motor of yours on the back of my wagon with the big rubber tires. The motor can drive one of the rear wheels through a couple of jackshafts and combination of speed-reducing V-pulleys so it will make the wagon just creep along. You'll also remember that I've taken all the remote control equipment out of the model tugboat while I'm refinishing the hull; so we can put this into the wagon and remote-control it. A solenoid operating a belt-tightener can serve as a clutch, and we can use one of those fractional-horsepower, reversible electric motors with a speed-reducing, power-amplifying gear train to steer the wagon. We can sit right here in the shade and send that wagon wherever we want to—up and down the whole beach."

"Well good, good, goody for us!" Carl said sarcastically; "but what's all that got to do with our locating the loot?"

"I'm coming to that. We'll mount the treasure-locator on the wagon with the search coil out in front, just clearing the surface of the sand. The audio beat-note signal that we hear in the earphones when something metallic appears near the search coil will be amplified, rectified, and the resulting current can be used to operate a sensitive relay which, in turn, will operate the clutch solenoid."

"You're getting through to me!" Carl said, with the enthusiasm that boys invariably feel for a really complicated Rube Goldberg device. "When the search coil passes over something metallic like, say, a five-hundred-dollar diamond-studded gold watch, the audio signal produced will trip the relay that will operate the solenoid that will stop the wagon. The gadget will just sit there like a faithful little old bird dog 'on point' until we leisurely stroll down to it, brush away the sand, pick up the watch, and toss it into the pillowcase full of other valuables we've already found."

"Well, let's go!" Jerry said, getting to his feet and brushing the loose sand from his knees and the seat of his trousers.

And go they did, just as fast as they could pedal their bicycles home. The heat that had seemed so oppressive when they had nothing to do was now entirely forgotten now as they worked out details of mounting the powerful little gasoline motor on the fat-tired coaster wagon. They connected up the remote control receiver and its reed-type actuator so that it could operate the steering mechanism and the simple clutch. Then they arranged the metal locator so that its hoop-shaped search coil was carried well out in front of the wagon two or three inches above the ground. With the motor and the jackshafts mounted behind the wagon and the probe coil sticking away out in front, the resulting ungainly appearance was something like that of an elongated king-sized insect . . . but the contraption worked!

Proof of this was had when Jerry fished a nickel from his pocket and recklessly tossed it out onto the middle of the lawn. They started up the self-powered remote-controlled treasure finder and sent it into action quartering back and forth across the yard. After having first turned up three rusty nails and an old belt buckle, it finally stopped with the search coil directly over the nickel. That was all the "testing" the boys needed. They immediately began coaxing Jerry's mother to drive them and their invention down to the beach in the station wagon, and did not let up until she agreed. Just as they were starting out the drive, Carl suddenly exclaimed: "Wups! Wait a minute. We're forgetting something."

He vaulted over the low fence between the two houses and disappeared into his own house. Almost immediately he came dashing back out waving an empty pillow-ease in which to dump their findings.

Once at the beach, the boys lost no time in putting their electronic beach buggy into action. The large tires kept the wheels of the wagon from cutting down into the sand, and the gasoline motor— thanks to the down-gearing—had an easy task propelling the vehicle along. At first the boys could not resist the temptation to send the treasure locator hither and thither along the beach to test out the operation of the remote control; but when it was found that this functioned perfectly, they settled down to directing the movement of the wagon in a regular pattern that eventually would cover the whole area of the beach in sight of what they dubbed their "command post."

The wagon had hardly gone a hundred yards when it came to a halt, and there was nothing leisurely about the way the boys dashed down to where it was sitting quietly put-put-putting away. As Carl eagerly brushed away the sand from beneath the search coil, he uncovered a little slip of tin foil from a stick of chewing gum, and instantly the wagon started chugging ahead, indicating that the bit of tin foil was what it had in mind.

A little disappointed, the boys started back to their command post, but before they reached it, the wagon stopped again. It had found another scrap of tin foil. To cut a long and painful story short, the metal locator found exactly twenty-three bits of tin foil in two hours—and it found nothing else! Actually, the boys were expending more energy running back and forth between their command post and the wagon than they would have used if they had simply carried the metal locator in the first place; but to them, of course, this fact was entirely irrelevant and beside the point.

Finally, Carl knelt in front of the search coil with the twenty-third scrap of tin foil in his hand and addressed it with an impassioned speech: "Now look, Tin-Foil Terry, you don't seem to get the idea. We're not looking for this kind of stuff. We can get all the tin foil we need. We want something like *this*." He placed some coins in the palm of his hand and held them directly in front of the search coil. "Now will you please, please get off this tin-foil binge you're on and go out there and find some of these pretty little engraved silver discs? Will you please?"

Again the boys trudged back to their command post, and the wagon chugged on down the beach. It did not hesitate until it reached the turn-around point, nor did it stop on the way back until it was almost directly in front of the boys. Then the motor speeded up a little as the solenoid clutch operated to stop the wagon.

"More tin foil," Carl grunted, heaving himself to his feet and starting across the hot sand toward the wagon.

"You can't be sure," Jerry said, optimistically, as he followed along. "We can hope, anyway."

And when Carl started brushing away the sand, it began to look as though his pep talk to Tin-Foil Terry had done some good, for no scrap of tin foil appeared, and the wagon stayed put, showing that whatever it was pointing to was still there.

"Dig deeper," Jerry suggested, as he knelt beside his pal.

Carl scooped away the sand to a depth of eight or ten inches, and suddenly his fingers touched a parcel wrapped in moldy, rotting, brown paper. He lifted it out of the hole and discovered that it was a heavy package some four inches wide by seven inches long by an inch thick. The wagon started up when the parcel was removed from beneath the coil, but Jerry stopped it by shorting out the spark plug of the motor.

"What the heck is it?" Jerry asked, with much curiosity.

"You got me, but I guess there's only one way to find out," Carl said, as he started unwrapping the decaying paper. Inside were two rectangular metal plates carefully wrapped separately in soft flannel. He handed one to Jerry to examine while he scrutinized the other.

"It's got a kind of design engraved on one of the flat surfaces," he said slowly, turning it so that the light made the design stand out. "There's a kind of cameo in the middle with a man's head on it, and there's some printing, too, but it's hard to make out because it's printed backwards."

"Mine's got a picture of some kind of big public building in the middle, and it has both letters and numbers printed on it. Let me see. Say, these must be printing plates for making mo—"

"Never mind what they are," a gruff voice commanded. "Just give them to me. They're mine."

The boys had been so intent on examining their find they had not heard the short dark man approaching in the soft sand. His beady black eyes glinted coldly out of his pasty white face as he held out a demanding hand for the plates.

"Hold it, Jake!" still another strange voice interrupted, and three men came running from behind one of the nearby dunes. At first the man they addressed as Jake looked as though he might run for it; but when he saw the guns in the hands of the approaching trio, he stood still.

"Couldn't wait any longer, huh, Jake?" one of the men inquired as he frisked the short dark man for a possible weapon.

"I'm clean," Jake grunted, "and I could have waited until you guys layin' out there in the dunes took root if these brats hadn't forced my hand."

"Hey, can anybody tell us what's going on?" Jerry piped up.

"This is Jake the Penman," the leader of the trio explained. "He's a well-known counterfeiter just out of prison after doing a stretch. But when the counterfeiting ring was broken up, the plates were never found. We put a tail on Jake as soon as he left prison, hoping he would lead us to where the plates were hidden; and, thanks to you boys and your—your—gadget there, he did. I'm not sure, but I rather think there will be a reward of some sort coming to you for helping to find the plates. But just as a matter of curiosity, would you mind telling us what that thing is? We've been lying out there watching you all afternoon, and none of us can figure it out."

Carl and Jerry, both talking at once, began an explanation of how the electronic beach buggy worked. When they finished, the leader of the three Federal agents shook his head as though to clear it of a bad dream.

"I still don't get it," he confessed; "but right here in my hand is the evidence that it works. Don't be surprised if some of the Treasury people want to examine it after I make my report. We might be able to use it in our business!"   —30—

ABETTING OR NOT?

Carl and Jerry were preparing to go on one of their electronic safaris. Equipment to be taken along was spread out on the workbench of their basement laboratory, and Jerry was carefully dividing it into two piles.

First he placed a 75-meter transceiver in each pile. These were followed by identical small dish-type reflector antennas and small collapsing tripod mounts to support them. Then he placed a small power supply in the pile next to him and a larger and much heavier combination power supply and modulator in the pile Carl was to carry.

Finally, two small chassis, each carrying what seemed to be a weird-shaped bit of brass plumbing clamped around the top of a metal tube, were divided among the growing stacks of equipment. The two chassis were not exactly alike for, in addition to the unusual-appearing tubes, one of them also had a conventional miniature glass tube mounted on it.

"These things look like they'd suck eggs," was Carl's disparaging remark as he examined the unusual pieces of equipment. "I've seen some odd-ball transmitters and receivers in my day, but these things are ridiculous."

"At 2400 megacycles, you can't expect conventional-looking transmitters and receivers," Jerry pointed out. "A wavelength at that frequency is only 12.5 centimeters long—or approximately 4.92 inches. Compare that with about 260 feet for a wavelength on 80 meters."

"What are these things that look like tubes crossed with bathroom fixtures?"

"Those are special ultra-high-frequency 'light-house' tubes with a cavity resonator clamped on top of them. The one-tube job is the

187

transmitter, while the other is the receiver—a superregenerative type with a separately quenched oscillator. The transmitter only puts out a maximum of a quarter of a watt, but these reflector-type antennas should give us enough gain to cover that quarter mile between Uncle Walt's and his neighbor up the highway."

"Why have we got to lug all this stuff clear out there? Why can't we just test it around here?"

"Because that's the closest place I know of where we can get a clear shot across that distance with absolutely nothing in the way, and where we can have power for our rigs at both ends. Uncle Walt lives right on a curve in the highway, and you can look from his front porch straight up the pavement to Mr. Arthur's porch. I'll operate the transmitter at Uncle Walt's, and you can work the receiver at Mr. Arthur's."

"What do we need the transceivers for, anyway?"

"We'll probably have to do a lot of adjusting of antenna direction, frequency, etc., to get maximum signal strength. Since we'll only have one transmitter and one receiver on the ultra-high frequency, we can only talk one way after we establish contact. Being able to talk back and forth on seventy-five while making adjustments will help a lot."

"Okay; so let's get going," Carl said, and he quickly exchanged the heavy power supply in his pile for the light one in Jerry's while the latter's back was turned.

The two boys loaded the equipment into the handlebar baskets they strapped on their bicycles *only* for occasions like this. (Ordinarily such accessories were considered "too sissy.") Carried along by their youthful enthusiasm, it required but a few minutes for them to pedal out to the farm of Jerry's uncle, Walter Bishop. Carl helped Jerry set up the transmitter and connect it to the power supply and modulator. The little dish-type antenna and reflector was perched on its tripod, and a short coaxial line ran down to the output fitting on the side of the cavity resonator.

Next, both boys rode on down the narrow path from the highway to Mr. Arthur's and set up the receiver on his porch. When Jerry was sure the receiver was working correctly, he took off the earphones and reached over and let them snap shut on Carl's head with a resounding "plop."

"Guess we're ready," he announced. "Use a single phone over one ear and leave the other free for use with the transceiver. The instant you hear my voice on the u.h.f. receiver, yell at *me* on the hand-held unit, for it will mean that I have the transmitting antenna pointed nearly at you. That beam will be very narrow, and we'll have to aim it right on the nose. Once we make contact, we can go ahead and align both transmitter and receiver antennas perfectly, checking back and forth with the transceivers; and then you can carefully tune the receiver to the exact transmitter frequency."

"I *can?*" Carl questioned sarcastically. "With what? I see nothing that looks like a tuning knob on this plumber's nightmare."

"You tune the receiver by turning this little screw right here on top of the cavity resonator with this long fiber screwdriver," Jerry explained; "and move it only a fraction of a turn at a time."

Having delivered this bit of advice, he hopped back on his bicycle and was soon at his uncle's place. After switching on the high-frequency transmitter, he pulled out the telescoping antenna of the war-surplus transceiver, which automatically turned it on. Holding the case so that the earphone was at his ear and the microphone in front of his lips, he pushed the transmit-receive switch covered with a waterproof rubber pouch on the side of the case.

"How do you read, W9EGV? This is W9CFI," he said.

"Loud and clear, W9CFI, from W9EGV," was the prompt answer.

"Okay; I'm going to start shooting at you. If you hear me, yell plenty loud, for I'll have to set the handie-talkie down on the floor while I'm fiddling with the antenna."

"Roger. Let's see if you can spray me with some of that u.h.f."

Jerry began carefully aiming the reflector at the porch of the white house up the road. For several seconds nothing happened, and then he heard a faint cry from the earphone of the handie-talkie sitting beside him. "Hold it!" Carl said, "You're knocking down the hiss in the receiver."

"Can you hear me?" Jerry asked into the microphone connected to the modulator of the u.h.f. transmitter.

"Sure can," came the answer. "Wups! You cut out for a minute, but it's okay again now."

As Carl said this, Jerry noticed a large black car with two men in it pull off the highway onto the path just next to his uncle's house. It was when this car had passed through the u.h.f. beam that Carl said the signal cut out momentarily. Jerry concluded the men had stopped to examine a map or something, and he and Carl went ahead with their experimenting.

It was not until two more cars pulled up opposite the first one that Jerry took more careful notice. One of the cars that just stopped was an ancient Model A Ford truck loaded with late-in-the-season watermelons. The driver was a little old man with a sharp-pointed white goatee; and from the way he popped from the cab and began waving his arms about, he was obviously quite excited about something. The unmistakable appearance of the other car, a state police patrol, gave a possible clue to the cause of his agitation.

"Hey, Carl," Jerry said into the mike, "you'd better come on down here and see what gives. Looks like it may get interesting."

Collapsing the antenna of the handie-talkie to shut it off, Jerry hurriedly left without thinking to shut *off* the u.h.f. transmitter. He had barely reached the parked cars before Carl came pumping up on his bicycle.

"I tell you," the little man was shouting, "that you and your fancy radar gadget are all wrong. You can't possibly drive that bucket-of-bolts at sixty-five."

"Take it easy, Pop," the big state trooper behind the wheel of the black car said good-humoredly. "This thing doesn't make mistakes. It said you were hitting sixty-five when you passed, and that's what you were doing. So we radioed ahead for Jim to stop you."

"Tell you what I'm gonna do," the man with the goatee offered. "If any one of the three of you can drive that Model A one mile over forty-five miles per hour, I'll give it to you and throw in the load of watermelons to boot!"

"Old timer, you've got yourself a deal," the youthful trooper named Jim said, as he slid out of his patrol car. "I always did want to drive one of those old cars my old man still insists is 'the best car Henry ever built.' If you got sixty-five out of that iron, so can I. I'll go back up the road a piece and come on by with the thing wide open so you boys can get a reading on me."

He got into the truck, and went off up the highway with the motor spluttering.

"**D**o you know how that radar thing works?" Carl whispered to Jerry.

"Sure. So would you if you had read the article about it in the May 1956 issue of *Popular Electronics*. It depends on the Doppler effect."

"I remember that from physics. It's an apparent change in frequency of a signal coming from a moving source as observed from a fixed position."

"Fine," said Jerry. "That's exactly right. The most common example is the apparent change in the pitch of a train whistle as it passes. When it's coming toward you, the pitch seems to increase; but as the train moves away, the pitch lowers. When the train is moving rapidly toward you, the sound waves are sort of bunched together and the pitch of the signal striking the ear is increased. When the whistle is moving away, the sound waves are stretched out, and the pitch seems lower. The radar gadget sends out a beam of u.h.f. signal that strikes the moving car and is reflected back to a receiver housed in the same unit with the transmitter.

"This reflected signal is mixed with the signal direct from the transmitter," Jerry continued, "and the difference between their frequencies is read by an audio frequency meter. The difference in frequency between the transmitted signal and the reflected signal depends directly on how fast the car reflecting the signal is moving. The faster it moves, the greater is the difference. At 100 miles per hour, the reflected signal will be shifted 731 cycles from the transmitter frequency of 2455 megacycles. Speeds below 100 miles per hour produce less shift. The audio frequency meter is calibrated in miles per hour for direct reading of speed."

"But where is the radar gadget?"

"Probably in the trunk of the black car. You can see the meter there on top of the dash. The signal is sent out and received back through a camouflaged hole in the metal lid of the trunk. All this car has to do is park along the highway and take speed readings. When a 'live prospect' shoots past, the radar car radios to a patrol car waiting about a mile down the highway, and he picks up the speeder. Well, here comes the truck; let's go over and see what kind of a reading it gives."

The boys moved over to the black car and watched the meter on the dash as the truck went spluttering by. The pointer rose sluggishly to a reading of thirty-five miles per hour.

"That's all that crate will do," Jim announced, as he drove back and parked the truck. "I had my foot clear down in the fan. My old man must have rocks in his head if he thinks that's a good car."

"I don't get it," the radar operator behind the wheel said to the other. "This thing never was wrong before. I still say we give the old gentleman a ticket—hey!" he broke off, "look at the meter."

Sure enough, the meter on the dash was jumping crazily about. Jerry's glance went from it to his Aunt Enid busily sweeping the immaculate front porch. (As every woman knows, a broom is a wonderful excuse for staying within earshot and eyesight of any interesting event!) As her broom nudged the coaxial cable, the dish antenna wobbled back and forth.

"Watch that meter a moment while I do something up on the porch," Jerry suggested to the men in the car. Running to the u.h.f. transmitter, he swept the invisible beam from the antenna back and forth across the trunk of the black car.

"That's what's doing it!" one of the men called. "What you got up there anyway?"

Carl and Jerry explained that the transmitter they were using was supposed to be in the 2300-2450 mc. ham band, but that since they had no extremely accurate frequency-measuring equipment at this frequency, the transmitter had drifted down very close to the 2455-mc. frequency of the radar transmitter. The difference in frequency was just enough to give a good reading on the speed indicator.

"Well, that's one for the book," the man behind the wheel said, tearing up the speeding ticket he had started to write. "Of all the places we had to set up our operation, we had to pick this one directly in the path of your beam. Pop, I'm sorry for all the hard time we've given you."

"That's all right, young man; we're all wrong at one time or another," the little man with the goatee said pleasantly; "but I feel I owe these boys a favor. How about giving you a lift back to town if you're ready to go? You can put your bikes in back."

The boys promptly took him up on the offer, and soon they were chugging down the road. After they had gone about a mile, the little old man took a cautious look in his rear-view mirror, then reached over to the right side of the dash and gave a shiny knob there a practiced turn counterclockwise. Instantly the popping motor smoothed out and the truck plunged forward on the road.

"These young whippersnappers don't savvy a combination choke and carburetor control any more than a redskin used to savvy the hindsight on a rifle," the old fellow said with a cackling laugh. "Fact is, most of the young ones don't know what a hand-choke is, let alone a dash-mounted carburetor control. When I saw that patrol car take out after me, I just leaned over and cut Betsy's gas down until she would barely run. That's why the officer could only get thirty-five out of her. Shucks, with her Fronty head and special camshaft, she'll hit seventy-five without a bit of trouble."

Carl and Jerry made no comment. When the old man let them out at their homes, he insisted that each accept a large watermelon.

As the old man drove off, Carl turned to his pal and said slowly: "Jer, I feel kind of funny. I'm not at all sure but that we helped defeat 'due process of law' today."

"Neither am I. On the other hand, maybe our transmitter did get into the act. We'll never know. Let's go in and eat some watermelon while we brood about it!" —30—

EEELECTRICITY!

November 1956

Carl was just arriving home after spending a short weekend vacation with an aunt and uncle in Chicago. He burst in the front door; yelled "Hi, Dad!", planted an awkward kiss on the bridge of his mother's nose, and then sailed out the back door, across the yards, and into the basement laboratory of his neighbor and best friend, Jerry Bishop.

Jerry was there all right, and he was just as glad to see his pal as Carl was to see him; but it was against the Code of Boyhood to show their feelings. Jerry hardly looked up as he grunted a greeting. To tell the truth, though, he was pretty busy trying to strap a squirming, wriggling *something* into the concave side of a short section of gutter trough. It kept slithering through the rubber gloves he was wearing.

"Holy cow, Jer, what is that thing?" Carl demanded. "Is it a snake?"

"Of course not, stupid. It's an eel that my uncle in the Navy sent me from South America. I want to make some tests on it. Put on that other pair of rubber gloves and help me fasten it in this trough."

"Not on your life!" Carl said emphatically as he backed toward the door. "I wouldn't touch that snaky-looking thing with a ten-foot pole, let alone my hands. Why on earth would your uncle send you something like that? Has he sprung his hatch?"

"Certainly not. This is not just an ordinary eel. In fact, it's not really an eel at all. Strictly speaking, it's an electric fish. My uncle says if I'm going to be an electronics engineer I should know about all forms of electricity; and electric fishes have been stirring electrons for thousands of years. Pictures of them appear in Egyptian tombs and they are mentioned in Aristotle's *Historia Animalium*. In addition to this so-called electric eel, there are five other fishes with shocking power: the torpedo or electric ray, the electric catfish, the star-gazer, the numb-fish, and the elephant-snout fish."

195

"Never mind the lecture, Professor," Carl said impatiently. "Just tell me what you are trying to do with Old Squirmy there."

"I want to strap him into this rubber-lined trough so I can find out something about the electric charge he emits. The rubber lining will prevent his being short-circuited by the metal trough. When I get him fastened down, I'll slide these little tin-foil strips underneath his body at different points to pick off the charge he emits. Then, by using the 'scope and the VTVM, I'll know if he has a.c. or d.c. wiring and how much voltage he puts out."

"You mean you don't have any idea what to expect? And are you wearing those rubber gloves because you don't want to touch the slimy thing or because you're afraid of being shocked?"

"To answer the last first, I'm wearing them cause I don't want to be shocked. A full-grown electric eel can put out a jolting five-hundred volts that can stun a horse or paralyze a man. Since eight feet is about as long as they get, and since this one is nearly five feet long, I'd guess he was full grown. He acts fully charged, too. An adult eel that puts out only three hundred volts is either sick or simply not letting himself go. Even a baby eel can deliver around 120 volts—as much voltage as there is in the a.c. house line."

"How do you know all this? You been boning up at the library?"

"Yes, and I got a lot more information from a story that appeared in the June-July, 1956, edition of a storage battery house organ called

Exide Topics that my uncle sent me. What I want to do right now is to double-check on some of the statements in that story."

"Looks like you've got Old Squirmy pretty well trussed up; so let's start double-checking," Carl suggested.

"Okay," Jerry agreed. "First let's see if this eel is a.c. or d.c. According to the eel experts, the electrical discharge he puts out is a series of rapid direct-current discharges in the form of short-duration pulses sent out at a rate of about four hundred per second. But these pulses are of such short duration, about two-thousandths of a second each, that the actual wattage output of an adult electric eel is only about forty watts."

"Then suppose we hook Buster here to a forty-watt bulb," Carl suggested.

"He's no good for lighting bulbs," Jerry explained. "Those pulses are too short to overcome the thermal lag of an incandescent bulb filament. Voltage has to be applied to such a filament for about one-fiftieth of a second before it begins to glow, and one of these pulses only lasts about one-tenth that long. But he could light a neon bulb, and I'm sure he'll make some interesting traces on our 'scope. I've got an idea about how to check his polarity, too. We'll simply run his output into this 0.5-microfarad capacitor and let him charge it up with his pulsating voltage. Then our VTVM connected across it will show his peak voltage and polarity."

As he talked, Jerry slipped one tin-foil-electrode beneath the tail of the eel and another beneath the center of his body. Leads from the electrodes went to the capacitor, and the VTVM was connected to read the voltage charging this capacitor.

"Three-hundred-and-fifty volts!" Carl announced. "And the way the pointer swings proves that Old Squirmy's tail is the negative pole of his battery and the front part of him is the positive pole."

"Watch the meter while I slide this front electrode back and forth," Jerry suggested. "I want to find where the front end of his generator actually is."

This method soon showed that the maximum voltage, four hundred and eighty volts, was obtained when the negative electrode was at the eel's tail and the positive electrode was at a point about a foot back from his head.

"That squares with what the books say," Jerry reported. "According to them, all of the critter's vital organs are in the front fifth of his body, and the rest is made up of 'electric tissue.'"

"Whatever that is."

"It's a flabby whitish jelly composed of 92% water. This stuff is organized into three pairs of electric organs. The eel can use one pair for a major discharge, one pair for a medium-size whammy, and the third pair for a small shock. Each organ is made up of smaller units separated by another kind of tissue that acts like the insulating separators in a storage battery. The electricity is actually produced in these smaller units. Each one produces about one-tenth of a volt. Somehow, in some way, the creature is able to connect these units in series to produce the high voltage discharges. But how he can throw thousands of 'switches' on and off several hundred times a second in perfect unison is still a mystery."

Jerry connected the leads from the electrodes to the horizontal input terminals of his 'scope and adjusted the linear sweep until he had two of the voltage spikes visible on the screen. Since the frequency of the eel's output was irregular, this pattern was not easy to hold, but a sweep frequency of around 200 cycles per second displayed two complete pulses. Once again this proved the books were right when they said that the eel put out about 400 discharges per second.

"For the rest of our experimenting," Jerry mused, "we should have the eel swimming freely about. Wonder where we can manage that? He's too big for a wash-tub."

Jerry and Carl looked deep into each other's eyes and saw the same thought. "Okay," Jerry said, "but you'll have to go ahead and make sure the coast is clear. Mom is deathly afraid of this thing, and if she saw us sneaking it into the bathroom, she would never set foot in there again."

Jerry gathered Old Squirmy, still strapped to the length of gutter trough, under his arm and cautiously followed Carl up the basement stairs. Jerry's mother, fortunately, was busy talking on the telephone and never noticed the boys tiptoeing past the door on their way to the second floor. Safely inside the bathroom, Carl started quietly filling the tub with water while Jerry made another trip to the laboratory for other equipment he wanted. When the tub was two-thirds full, the eel was released inside it. He seemed to enjoy his freedom and went slithering around on the bottom of the tub in graceful coils. Jerry separated the earpieces of a pair of headphones and handed one to Carl.

"Listen!" he said, as he dipped the metal-tipped ends of the headphone cord in the water. Clearly heard in the phones was a static-like noise. When the eel was quiet, this noise subsided; but as soon as it started to move, the noise returned.

"Any time he is moving," Jerry explained, "the electric eel gives off a series of weak discharges. These serve two purposes: First, they warn enemies to keep their distance; and second, they form a kind of radar that enables the eel—which is virtually blind when it is adult—to seek out its prey."

"Wait a minute!" Carl interrupted. "I'm not so dumb that I don't know a radar system consists of a receiver as well as a transmitter. I'll admit Old Squirmy has a dan-dan-dandy low-frequency transmitter; but then where's his receiver?"

"He's got one all right, according to the books," Jerry replied. When one eel in a tank discharges, all the other eels come to the spot, apparently to horn in on the result. Obviously they know when one of their fellows is trying to stun something and can judge very nicely where the current is coming from. But now let's see if we can prove this with the eel-caller I've built up. It's a blocking oscillator that produces sharp spikes of voltage over a frequency range that is adjustable from about 500 to 2000 cycles per second. The output of the oscillator drives an output tube so as to produce pulses of very respectable amplitude across these two electrodes. Let's place the electrodes in the water at this end of the tub and see if we can sweet-talk him into coming over."

Carl did as he was told, and Jerry began varying the frequency of the blocking oscillator. As a certain frequency was reached, the eel on the bottom of the tub began to stir and swim directly to the electrodes. When they were transferred to the opposite end of the tub, he immediately moved toward them.

"Old Squirmy's receiving frequency seems to be around 800 cycles per second," Jerry announced.

"Say! That thing really puts the come-hither on him," Carl said enthusiastically. "We ought to patent it."

"We're a little too late," Jerry told him. "Eel hunters in South America are already using earphones to locate electric fish and then are employing eel-callers something like this one to lure them into their traps. But to get back to his built-in radar, by means of it the electric eel can move straight toward his prey and can detect a variation of just a few inches. What's more, he can tell instantly if his prey is moving and can make allowances for that movement."

"You know," Carl mused, "that's all pretty wonderful when you stop to think about it. Here we think of electricity itself as being quite modern, but that ugly creature resting there on the bottom of the tub and his ancestors have been using electricity for thousands of years. What's more, they've been using it in ways that we think of as being ultra-modern. Since electric eels talk to each other by means of their electric discharges, we must admit that they are equipped with wireless telephones. Those same discharges are employed as a compact, efficient, and highly effective weapon to secure food and to combat enemies. Finally, the lowly eel has been quietly using radar— which we did not discover until the last war—for countless centuries. It kind of makes you wonder if man—in spite of all his scientific development and progress—is so doggone smart as he thinks he is, doesn't it?"

"It certainly does," Jerry agreed, "and I think my uncle had something like that in mind when he sent me the eel and told me to study it. When we work with electricity that is man-produced by batteries and generators and so on, we sort of take it for granted and forget how magic it really is, but when you see electricity being generated within the living tissue of a live creature such as this, all the wonder and mystery of it sweeps over you, and you are glad that you intend to make a lifetime study of it." —30—

EXTRA-SENSORY PERCEPTION

December 1956

It was a bleak Saturday afternoon in early December, and Carl and Jerry were sitting in Jerry's basement doing absolutely nothing. This was most unusual, for the two were generally busy at something or other. But there they were: Jerry sprawled on the old leather-covered couch along the wall; and Carl sitting across the workbench, elbows on knees and chin propped on hands.

"Hey, Jer," Carl finally drawled, "do you have trouble staying awake in that second period assembly?"

"Sure do," Jerry said with a reminiscent yawn. "Guess neither of us needs to do much studying in there, and there's nothing else to do. Even the surrounding scenery is no good. Did you notice the girls who sit on both sides of me? Real beasts!"

"Naw, I don't pay any attention to girls," Carl said, just a trifle too emphatically, "but I wish we had something to do in there. If we could just talk to each other some way—"

He stopped speaking as Jerry suddenly swung his feet to the floor and sat upright on the creaking couch. "That's an idea!" Jerry exclaimed. "Why don't we build a couple of little transmitters and receivers and chew the fat during that period instead of wasting time?"

"Well, I dunno," Carl said doubtfully. "We'd have to use code instead of phone, and it would have to be doggoned quiet code at that. You know how still that crabby old Miss Dean keeps things in that study hall. I've seen her send kids to the office just for shuffling their feet."

"Yeah, that's right," Jerry said thoughtfully. "We couldn't use earphones, even the hearing-aid type. She would certainly spot something like that."

"If we just had some system so we could *feel* the signals instead of hear them—" Carl started to say.

"That's it" Jerry interrupted. "We'll use a low-frequency note to modulate the transmitter. The receiver will amplify this and feed it to a diaphragm-type earphone with the diaphragm taped right against a sensitive portion of the skin. With a little practice, we should be able to interpret the buzzing sensation produced by dots and dashes just as well as we could if we were hearing an audible note."

"What kind of transmitter and receiver will we need?"

"Transistor types in both cases, in the interest of small size and low battery drain," Jerry promptly said. "I think the receiver should be a regenerative detector with a couple of stages of audio behind it to furnish plenty of drive to the earphone—or perhaps we should call it a 'skin-phone.' The transmitter will consist of an r.f. oscillator modulated by a low-frequency audio oscillator. We'll key this audio oscillator and let the r.f. generator run all the time. Since we'll only be working over distances of a few dozen feet, no antennas will be necessary,"

"What kind of a key can we use?"

"A tiny one made with a couple of pieces of spring brass will be good enough. The leads from this can run through a shirt sleeve so that the key can be concealed in the palm of the hand and worked by simply squeezing the contacts together. After all, we won't be sending thirty-five words per minute. When the key isn't in use, it can be slipped back inside the shirt sleeve."

"Well, let's get started!" Carl suggested, hopping off the bench. "I want to have this thing ready to go by Monday, and if we don't run into some bugs that need ironing out, it will be the first time."

This time was no exception. The receivers gave no trouble, but the transmitters made up for it. Even at the low frequency used— around 550 kilocycles— the oscillators were sluggish. They tried several circuits before they found one that was stable in performance and would accept modulation from the low-frequency oscillator. Finally, though, by late Sunday afternoon the problems were all apparently licked, and the boys were ready for a trial. Each boy had a small earphone, with its cap removed, taped to the inside of his upper right arm so that the face of the diaphragm was flat against his skin. A tiny transmitter was carried in one shirt pocket, a small receiver in the other.

"Are you ready?" Jerry asked, as he looked across the laboratory at Carl.

"Fire at will!" Carl answered.

Jerry started squeezing the "key" concealed in the palm of his hand, and Carl flinched and began to giggle. "Hey, that tickles!" he announced, "but I can make out your 'CQ' all okay. 'Try something else now."

Jerry began tapping out the dots and dashes to ask: "Can you read this?" And he jumped in turn as Carl promptly came back with the "di-dah-dit" of "received okay" followed by the "dah-di-dah-dit" that means "yes" in the code used by amateurs. In the few minutes remaining before supper, the boys found that they could easily work each other up to about a hundred feet apart. Then they had to lay their new playthings aside.

The next morning their mothers did not have the least trouble getting them started off for school; but oddly enough, the boys did not walk together as they usually did. Instead, they went down opposite sides of the street, with faraway looks in their eyes and their right hands working spasmodically.

It was during the second period study hall that they had the opportunity to give their brainchild the acid test. As soon as the bell had rung and everything was quiet, Miss Dean started her gimlet-eyed stroll through the aisles. Just as she walked past Carl's desk, Jerry tapped out: "What a sour-puss!" He did not need to feel the buzzing acknowledgment against his arm; Carl's heaving shoulders told clearly that he had got the message.

The boys had a real picnic during the study period sending messages back and forth. Every boy is a lodge brother at heart, and the fact that what they were doing was secret and entirely unnoticed by others in the room added tremendously to the flavor of the accomplishment. Time went very fast, and just before the end of the period, the voice of the principal boomed through the loudspeaker on the wall announcing: "Instead of going to your next class or study hall, all students will proceed to the auditorium for a special program to be presented by Professor Karns of the psychology department of our state university."

The boys' study room was directly across the hall from the auditorium; consequently Carl and Jerry were in the vanguard of the thundering herd that surged through the doors of the auditorium. As a result, they were seated in the second row from the stage when the curtains parted. A dapper man wearing *pince-nez* glasses stepped to the proscenium and said:

"Good morning, students. The program that you will see now is going to be a little unusual. To some of you it will be quite interesting. Others will find it dull. What you think of it does not really matter. You are going to be permitted to take part in an experiment in what is known as 'Extra Sensory Perception.' There is a growing belief in some quarters that a certain amount of information can be transferred from one mind to another without the aid of any of the usual senses. To check the validity of this belief, our psychology department is conducting experiments, such as the one in which you are about to participate, at various high schools and keeping a careful record of the results. Out of these experiments, we hope to arrive at some definite conclusions as to whether there actually is such a thing as 'ESP' or not.

"To go on with the experiment, I shall need an assistant. Experience has taught me that it is useless to call for volunteers from a high school group; so I'll draft one of you. Let me see now. The tall young man wearing glasses in the second row looks like a bright chap. Will you please come up here, young man?"

Hands on all sides, even those of his buddy, boosted a reluctant Carl to his feet and shoved him out into the aisle. He walked awkwardly up the steps to the stage and faced the professor.

"Don't look so frightened," the professor said jovially. "This is not going to hurt a bit. You are familiar with the names of a deck of playing cards?"

"Yes," Carl said in a small hoarse voice.

"Fine! I want you to stand right here at the front of the stage facing the audience. On the elevated screen at the back of the stage I'll show a card at a time with this projector. As each card shows on the screen, I want all of the students to concentrate on its name and suit as hard as they can for five full seconds. At the end of that time I shall strike this little bell, and I want you to name the first card that comes into your mind. For example, you may say, 'ace of diamonds' or 'nine of clubs,' or whatever card is in your mind at the second you hear the bell. What we shall be trying to do is to transfer the knowledge of the card directly from the mind of the audience to your mind. A young lady back in the wings—she is too pretty to have on the stage because she would distract attention from the experiment—will keep a careful record of each card shown and the cards you name.

"But let me warn the audience not to expect too many correct identifications. The odds against your correctly naming even one card are tremendous, and it is against these mathematical odds that we are competing. If you can better the law of probability by just a little, it will be significant."

Jerry was watching Carl closely, and he saw the latter's mouth draw into a straight line that meant he was not taking at all kindly to the glib man beside him. Jerry did not like him either. He sounded too much as if he were trying to be "cute," as though he were talking down to his youthful audience.

The lights were lowered, and suddenly a huge queen of spades appeared on the screen above and behind Carl. With a sudden inspiration, Jerry squeezed the little brass contacts already held in the moist palm of his hand to spell out "QS." As he finished the last dot, the bell tinkled and Carl promptly said in a loud voice: "Queen of spades!"

"An astounding, auspicious beginning!" the professor exclaimed. "Let's try another."

He flashed the seven of hearts on the screen. Jerry immediately tapped out "7H," and Carl called out: "Seven of hearts!" the instant he heard the sound of the bell.

"This places too much of a strain on coincidence," the dapper man said in a suspicious, harried voice. "Maybe you can see some reflection of the screen, or perhaps some smart aleck in the audience is signaling you in some fashion. Would you mind letting me blindfold you?"

"Go right ahead," Carl said in return.

After a moment of indecision, the scientist won over the fashion plate, and the professor removed the handkerchief that was peeping meticulously from his breast pocket and securely blindfolded Carl. Then he went back to his projector and flashed the jack of spades on the screen. Carl easily translated the dots and dashes of "JS" buzzing against his arm into the name of the card. Desperately, the scientist flashed card after card on the screen, and Carl called off each one correctly.

By this time the professor was so disturbed and puzzled that he had forgotten all about his appearance. Frantic fingers run through his hair had left it tousled. He tugged at his shirt collar as he walked slowly around Carl, looking at him with deep, incredulous interest.

"I just can't believe it!" he muttered. "One-hundred-percent correct identification! Young man, can you explain how you perform this feat?"

"I just did what you told me to do," Carl said blandly. "I simply called out the card that was in my mind when the bell sounded. Guess it must be a kind of telepathy, or something."

"'Or something' is right," Professor Karns fervently agreed. "I must take you down to the university with me and give a demonstration of your phenomenal ability to my colleagues."

"Aw, I don't think I could do that," Carl objected, as he started backing toward the steps leading down from the stage. "I don't like to mess around with this sort of thing. Makes me feel kind of creepy."

"But you owe it to science!" the professor argued. "If we can repeat this experiment, my account of it will appear in every scientific journal in the world."

"I'll think about it," Carl said, hastily going down the steps.

The assembly was dismissed, and as Carl and Jerry walked along the hall Jerry whispered: "That was a lot of fun, but it certainly means that we'll not dare wear these contraptions to school again. And don't ever breathe a word about them. If it is ever found out how we helped ESP, you and I are going to be the guests of honor at the darndest tar-and-feathering party you ever saw; and I can just see Professor Karns ladling out the hot tar right now!" —30—

www.ingramcontent.com/pod-product-compliance
Lightning Source LLC
Chambersburg PA
CBHW020423180626
46812CB00003B/1127